DUTTON CHILDREN'S BOOKS
Published by the Penguin Group
Penguin Group (USA) LLC
375 Hudson Street
New York, New York 10014

USA/Canada/UK/Ireland/Australia/New Zealand/India/South Africa/China

penguin.com
A Penguin Random House Company

LIBRARY OF CONGRESS CATALOGING-IN-PUBLICATION DATA
Cummings, Priscilla, date, author.
Cheating for the chicken man / Priscilla Cummings.
p. cm.

Summary: High school freshman Kate has a lot on her mind, what with taking care of her
heart-broken mother and looking after the family chicken farm in Maryland, but she promised
her dying father to look after her older brother who is just back from juvenile detention—and this
year that seems to involve paying off the bullies at school by doing their school work.

ISBN 978-0-525-42617-2 (hardcover)

1. Cheating (Education)—Juvenile fiction. 2. Bullying—Juvenile fiction. 3. Brothers and
sisters—Juvenile fiction. 4. Responsibility—Juvenile fiction. 5. High schools—Juvenile fiction. 6.
Families—Maryland—Juvenile fiction. 7. Poultry farms—Maryland—Juvenile fiction.
[1. Cheating—Fiction. 2. Bullying—Fiction. 3. Brothers and sisters—Fiction.
4. Responsibility—Fiction. 5. High schools—Fiction. 6. Schools—Fiction.
7. Chickens—Fiction. 8. Family life—Fiction. 9. Farms—Fiction.]
I. Title.
PZ7.C9149Cj 2015
[Fic]—dc23
2014036264

Printed in the United States of America

1 3 5 7 9 10 8 6 4 2

Text set in Chaparral Pro
Designed by Theresa Evangelista

FOR HANNAH

CHEATING

for the

CHICKEN MAN

PRISCILLA CUMMINGS

Dutton Children's Books

An imprint of Penguin Group (USA) LLC

CONTENTS

The color of truth is gray.
—André Gide

~1~
DAY IS DONE

The funeral was on a warm October day with a high blue sky and a single wispy white cloud that drifted, waiting like an angel, Kate thought. Her mother said they had been to Arlington National Cemetery before, when Kate's grandfather was buried, but that was ten years ago, when Kate was only two, and she didn't remember. Standing outside her grandmother's car, Kate brought her hopeful gaze down from the sky and took in the cemetery around them, gathering a little bit more strength from the beauty of the majestic trees that had turned the yellows and reds of autumn and shaded the endless rows of identical white tombstones.

Her grandmother had suggested that Kate and her five-year-old sister, Kerry, wear simple summer dresses because it was so warm, and carry a sweater in case it got cold later. So Kate had chosen a favorite blue jersey with tiny white dots and wore the ladybug earrings her father had bought for her a year ago at the county fair. She reached up to touch an earlobe while her mother and grandmother finished collecting things from the car. It was a bittersweet memory, that fair, because it was the last time Kate could remember her father going anywhere fun.

After the car was locked, Kate and her family set out across the parking lot to a special building. Kate was surprised to see so many people. Tourists, she guessed, judging by their cameras and the casual way they were dressed in shorts, jeans, and T-shirts, their outfits topped off by baseball caps and sun visors. Could they tell that Kate and her family were different? That they were here to actually bury someone? Kate desperately hoped these people wouldn't be allowed at the funeral. It didn't seem right and only added to the anxiety she already felt.

After a short walk to the administration building, they were directed to a special room, which, thankfully, was just for them. Although Kate knew her older brother, J.T., couldn't be there, because Mom had forbidden it, her eyes nevertheless swept the room, just to be sure. When she spied Uncle Ray and Aunt Helen standing nearby, talking with familiar neighbors, Kate took in and let out a deep breath. Then suddenly, her best friend, Jess, was there, opening her arms.

Kate embraced her. "I didn't know you were coming," she murmured into the mass of Jess's red curls. She and Jess had been best friends since first grade, when they met at a home-schoolers' field trip to the Smithsonian National Museum of Natural History. They were the only two brave enough to hold a giant hissing cockroach in their hands that day.

"Of course we came," Jess said. "We're all going to miss your dad."

When the two girls released each other, Jess asked, "Are you doing okay?"

Kate slowly lifted her shoulders in a shrug, but thought, *Not really*.

Jess leaned in close. "I saw Brady Parks last night."

Kate's eyebrows went up. "You did?"

"I ran into him at the 7-Eleven."

Kate felt her heart squeezed yet again. It had been weeks since Kate had seen Brady. She had known him all her life. He lived next door, after all. He was a year older than Kate and best friends with her brother. Who knew when it happened, but at some point, probably sixth grade, a year after she entered public school, she had secretly developed a crush on Brady. No one but Jess ever suspected.

"Brady said to tell you he was really sorry to hear about your dad," Jess told her. "He said that he and his parents would have come to the funeral, but they were afraid it might not go over so well."

Kate's eyes widened even further, but she understood. It was Brady who had reported Kate's brother and another friend to the police after a prank ended tragically with the death of a little boy. For weeks afterward—up until the day J.T. was sent to a juvenile detention center—the boys didn't see each other, and didn't text or talk. Kate always figured they wouldn't want anything to do with each other ever again. And she just assumed that included her as well.

"Are you sure?" Kate asked. "Brady said that?"

Jess nodded, but there wasn't time to discuss it any further, or think about it just then, because an army officer was directing them on to the ceremony.

Back outside, a slight breeze stirred the sultry air. Kate glanced downhill, across the Potomac River at the city of Washington, DC, where she was surprised to see in a straight line, the Lincoln Memorial, the Washington Monument, and the Capitol. It made Kate proud that her father had fought in the Gulf War, and another wave of sadness rolled over her.

People attending her father's funeral got back in their cars and drove in a small caravan to a different location. Kate hadn't realized the cemetery was so big, although she knew from her grandmother that several funerals were taking place the same day, as many as twenty. Some were even happening at the same time, in different parts of the cemetery. The Tylers had had to wait three weeks for a burial date, and it had given Kate nightmares, the thought of her father on hold in "cold storage," awaiting his turn to be buried. But in the end, the delay had given them some extra time, which turned out to be a good thing.

Kate later wrote in her journal.

We parked again. I told Kerry she had to leave her Barbie in the car. Then we walked the rest of the way. Grandma and Uncle Ray stayed with Mom. Sometimes it looked like they were holding her up. Kerry held tight to my hand. Everyone followed the four black horses that pulled a caisson with Dad's casket on it. It was sunny and getting hotter. I wished I had my sunglasses. The horses' hooves clip-clopped on the hard asphalt of the narrow hilly road. Once we had to step around a fresh, steaming pile of horse manure.

When we arrived at the gravesite, a small military band was already there. An open-sided tent provided shade for two rows of chairs that were covered with the same color blue velvet as the inside of J.T.'s trumpet case. Probably just a coincidence, but I did wonder if it was a sign.

The chaplain talked about Dad. He said Jacob Tyler was an honest, hardworking man who loved his wife, Angela, and his children, J.T., Kate, and Kerry. When Kerry heard her name, she leaned against my side and we squeezed hands again. It made me feel good that J.T. got mentioned. My brother practically ran the farm after Dad got so sick he couldn't work. But I worried all over again about what was going to happen to the family business and to us now that our father was gone.

When the chaplain talked about how much my father loved the Chesapeake Bay, where he'd grown up and lived most all his life, I saw Uncle Ray cover his eyes. The chaplain didn't talk about this, but I remembered how Dad and Uncle Ray, who was a waterman, liked to go fishing every so often before dawn and how sometimes Dad would bring home a huge rockfish with glistening scales that filled the entire kitchen sink. How come we didn't take Dad out on the bay one last time so he could feel the breezes he loved so much? We knew he didn't have long to live. We could have bundled him up in quilts and taken him out on Uncle Ray's workboat.

Kate's journal description of the funeral ended there because after the chaplain finished and led them in prayer, the ceremony had shifted gears and Kate didn't want to write about the rest. She didn't want there to be a written record of what she had done.

"Present arms!" an officer barked in a loud, crisp voice. Everyone stood. Seven soldiers who were lined up on the hill before them raised their rifles angled toward the sky.

"Prepare to fire!" the voice called out. Kerry, who had folded her hands for the prayer, reached out for Kate's fingers.

"Ready . . . aim . . . fire!"

Seven rifles fired at the same time, cracking open the sky. Kerry jumped, grabbing Kate's hand with both of hers, and startled birds scattered, their wings beating the air. Three times, the order rang out. Three times, the soldiers fired simultaneously, their volleys honoring her father's military service.

When the guns fell silent, Kerry's grip let up, but Kate held her breath with anticipation because she knew that, in a moment, a bugle—or a trumpet—would sound taps.

Her mouth went dry as she counted to herself: One . . . two . . . three . . .

Day is done . . .

The poignant and familiar opening notes rang out somberly.

Gone the sun . . .

People shifted uncomfortably. Uncle Ray put an arm around the shoulders of Kate's mother. A lump formed in Kate's throat while she tried to figure out where the trumpeter stood.

From the hills . . .

Somewhere behind them.

From the lake . . .

All those years of Brownie Girl Scouts. Kate couldn't help but hear the words in her head as taps was played.

From the skies . . .

Neither could she help but turn her head to look. He was hard to see, but through misty eyes, Kate discerned her brother's tall, lean profile on the crest of a small hill about fifty yards behind them. He wore black pants and a dark jacket, and Kate could tell that his hair had been cut really short. The silver instrument in his hand glinted in the late-afternoon sun. Miss Laurie, his counselor at the juvenile detention center, must have made time in his schedule for him to practice. Good for J.T., Kate thought, sighing with relief. A subtle, secret smile slowly graced her lips.

All is well . . .

On the song's highest note, Kate slowly faced forward again. She didn't think anyone else had looked back, the way she had. So no one else in her family would ever know.

Safely rest . . .

A tear slid down her cheek.

God is nigh . . .

As the trumpet's last note lingered in the still air, Kate held her breath against a wall of overwhelming sadness but took comfort in knowing that not only had she honored her father's dying wish, she had protected her brother as well.

Miss Laurie, I'm calling for my mother again. . . . She wants you to handle it this way because J.T. being there, it might upset some people. . . .

The lie had been so easy.

A small lie, yes, but so what if you did it for your family?

After taps, two soldiers lifted the American flag that covered her father's coffin and straightened it with a dramatic snap before folding it, over and over, into a neat triangle. Like a reflection in a mirror, the two soldiers wore identical crisp blue uniforms. Their eyes connected as if by rods, their faces stern and expressionless as the folding flag drew them together, step by step. The flag was presented to Kate's mother by the chaplain on bended knee. "On behalf of the president of the United States . . . a grateful nation. . . ."

When Kate turned to look again, the crest of the hill was empty. J.T. was gone, having quietly, and quickly, disappeared. As they had discussed.

Kate had done what she had to do, and no one else knew. No one else would ever need to know.

Only later did Kate look back on her father's funeral and wonder if that kind of thinking was where her own downfall began.

~2~
SEARCHING

"What happens next?" Kerry asked, tugging on the skirt of Kate's dress.

"I think it's over," Kate told her. "We walk back to our cars."

"Are we going home, then?" She pouted. "I want my kitty. I want Jingles."

"I don't know, Kerry," Kate said, distracted. She glanced at the hill behind them to see if it was still empty. "I'm not sure if we go straight home or not."

Suddenly, a commotion up ahead had people scrambling.

Kate glimpsed her mother, crumpled on the ground, with Uncle Ray bending over her. Pulling Kerry along, Kate began to run toward them.

Aunt Helen stopped her. "Kate, let me take Kerry," she said.

"No!" Kerry whimpered. "I'm scared. What's wrong with Mommy?" But Kate released her sister into Aunt Helen's arms and rushed on.

Was it a heart attack? Kate's own heart pounded high in her

chest. Her mother's hand was up at her throat, like she was struggling to breathe. Was she going to die the same day they buried her father? Kate's hand covered her mouth. Could something like that really happen to people?

Uncle Ray stood up. "It's okay," he told the chaplain, who was pulling out a cell phone. Her uncle's voice was surprisingly calm. "You don't need to call for help. It's a panic attack. She's had them before."

"He's right," said Kate's grandmother, who was kneeling on the ground beside Kate's mother. She looked up at the two men. "She needs to focus on her breathing. Give us some space. *Please*."

The chaplain turned to the gathering crowd and held up his arms. "She needs space! Some privacy, please!"

People stopped and, haltingly, moved away. Kate brought her hand down, but stayed kneeling beside her grandmother.

"She'll be all right, hon," Grandma said, tapping Kate's knee before leaning over Kate's mother. "Angela, a deep breath. That's it! In on five. Now hold for two."

This was all new to Kate. A panic attack? Breathing and counting? Kate had thought she knew her mother's secrets. But apparently not.

It took Grandma two hours to drive from the cemetery to the Tylers' home on the Eastern Shore of Maryland. By the time they arrived, it was late afternoon, and Kate's exhausted mother went straight to bed. The two girls changed into jeans, while Kate's grandmother fixed them grilled cheese sandwiches for dinner. Kerry was allowed to keep the cat on her lap while they ate, and no one spoke much. Even Tucker, J.T.'s border collie, seemed to pick up on the mood and lay quietly beneath the kitchen table, surrounded by their feet.

A low rumble and the grating sound of a large truck shifting gears distracted them. Kate pushed back her chair and, flip-flops flapping, went to the living room picture window that faced the road. "Darn!" she muttered, disappointed to see a gray-colored school bus crunching over the long oyster-shell driveway.

"What is it?" Grandma asked when Kate returned to the kitchen.

"The new chicks are here," Kate told her.

"Oh, dear," her grandmother sympathized. "They wouldn't even give you the day off for your father's funeral."

"It's fine, Grandma. No big deal," Kate said, quickly putting her best face on it. "We knew they were coming; I just forgot. Uncle Ray already asked me to do it. He had to get home for that plumber, remember? Something happened to their well."

"Well, bless your heart," Grandma said, reaching for a napkin. "Here, take the sandwich with you."

Kate waved her off. "It's okay," she said, sitting on the floor to pull on old sneakers. "I'd rather eat when it's done."

When she was ready, Tucker scrambled through the back door before Kate and rushed across the yard, barking at the bus-turned-delivery truck as it beeped and backed up to a long, low building. VALLEY SHORE CHICKEN FARMS was written in big black letters beneath the bus windows. This was the business that hatched the chicks and delivered them to the Tylers to raise. Every nine weeks, 54,400 chicks were brought to the farm. Funny, but after all these years, the company's name suddenly struck Kate as absurd. There were no mountains on the Eastern Shore of Maryland—it was flat as a pancake—so how could there be valleys? But it sounded nice, didn't it? Valleys and shores. If people only knew, Kate thought.

The bus stopped, and with it, the irritating *beep, beep, beep.*

First things first.

"Tucker!" Kate called, clapping her hands. When the dog trotted to her side, she took hold of his collar and gently led him into a toolshed off the tractor garage. "Just for a little bit, okay?" The dog sat and looked up at her. "No bark. Stay!" she ordered, showing him the palm of her hand.

After closing the shed door, she walked across the yard to where the bus had parked at one of the two chicken houses. She entered a number combination that unlocked the door and stepped aside so the deliverymen could begin unloading plastic trays full of newly hatched baby chicks. Each tray held about a hundred chicks, and both men carried about ten trays stacked one on top of the other, like a tall and very noisy bread delivery.

"Good afternoon," Kate said politely.

"Afternoon there, young lady," one of the men said. He was chewing tobacco—a wad of it made one cheek bulge—and after he greeted her, he turned his head to spit a dark stream of juice into the dust.

Uncle Ray had spent almost a week getting ready for the baby chicks. Using a backhoe, he had scraped the floors clean of caked manure, then hosed everything off, stocked the feeders with smaller, starter feed, and freshened the water supply. Even though the early fall weather was still warm, the nights were cool, and a propane heater had been blowing hot air into

She didn't write about the social scene at school and how the other girls seemed to be moving a lot faster than she was, some of them wearing heavy eye makeup and gossiping about which boys were cute and weekend parties where there was beer. Not that Kate was totally disinterested in parties or boys. But in all honesty, Kate still thought the epitome of cute was the poster on her closet door of a baby black rhino. "The ears especially," she told Jess, who totally agreed.

Thank goodness for Jess, Kate thought. They still liked a lot of the same things. Beyond that, Jess was always so upbeat, too, insisting, for example, that Kate was lucky because she never broke out and didn't need braces while Kate still saw herself as hopelessly plain. A real Plain Jane. A girl on the skinny side who hated tight clothes, so everything she wore puckered or hung loose. A girl with unexciting brown hair that hung in erratic waves to her shoulders unless she straightened it—and she hated straightening it. A girl who seldom broke out, true, but whose skin was so sensitive she never tanned, only burned and got red.

Only once did Kate write about her mother's troubling behavior. (*She had another panic attack yesterday. She collapsed on the front steps when she was on her way to the doctor with Grandma. Now she won't drive, and ever since that last panic attack, she hasn't wanted to leave the house, not even to go to church.*) Nothing prompted J.T. to write back. Didn't he care anymore?

Finally, in her last letter, Kate let J.T. know that her birthday had come and gone in April. (*I'm thirteen now! A teenager—yikes! Kids at school still tease me about being the class baby, but that's because Jess and I skipped a year when we entered public school, remember?)* Again, no response from J.T.

Nine months J.T. had been away. It went so slowly—and yet, so quickly, too. Because suddenly here she was, Kate thought, sitting in the school gym, at the end-of-the-year eighth-grade assembly. Tomorrow J.T. would be home. In three months, she and J.T. would be in high school together. Maybe by then, life would be back to normal.

"Our next award goes to Kate Tyler!" Mr. Coburn announced, startling Kate. Her heart jumped—she hadn't been paying attention—and just then, the microphone screeched, making everyone cringe before the principal continued.

"Not only did Kate write some beautiful poems and insightful essays this year, but she conceived the idea of Corsica Middle School's first literary magazine, *Wingspan*, to promote creative writing. Thirty-two of you Herons were published and left your tracks with poems, illustrations, and essays in the first editions of *Wingspan*. Kate worked closely with faculty adviser Heather Landon on all three issues. Let's give them both a big hand!"

Jess elbowed Kate, then squeezed her arm and clapped enthusiastically. Kate, embarrassed by the attention, reluctantly stood, then picked her way down the crowded bleachers and padded across the wood floor. Mrs. Landon gave her a hug, and then the principal shook her hand and gave her a certificate along with a Blue Heron mug filled with Hershey Kisses.

"We need to celebrate the end of school," Jess said as the two girls walked toward their bus. "How about if I talk my mom into taking us over to the Annapolis mall? We could watch a movie and get frozen yogurt. We could go shopping for sunglasses!"

"This weekend?" Kate was not sharing Jess's excitement. "That would be great, Jess, but remember, J.T.'s coming home tomorrow morning."

Jess grimaced. "Oh, my gosh, Kate. I *totally* forgot."

Just then the two girls were jostled and separated, then forced into a haphazard line to board the bus.

Kate hadn't forgotten J.T. was coming home. She had seen her brother only once since the funeral seven months ago. The week before Christmas, Kate's grandmother had driven them out to the detention center. The journey was long—six hours—because snow flurries had slowed them down.

Their visit took place in the prison's small cafeteria. J.T. couldn't take any gifts or food back to his dormitory, but he was allowed to eat during the visit, so Kate and her grandmother had stopped at a Subway shop along the way and picked up J.T.'s favorite sandwich, along with a bag of potato chips, a giant chocolate chip cookie, and a soda. Kate remembered thinking her brother would be excited to see them and ravenous, practically inhaling his favorite food, but he was neither. He was quiet as he sat across from them and seemed tired, taking only a couple bites before he wrapped the meatball sub back up and told Kate to eat it on the way home.

"Those sunglasses can wait," Jess said when she and Kate found a seat together on the bus. "Don't worry about it."

Kate turned, a slight frown wrinkling her brow, before she remembered what Jess was talking about.

The next morning, Uncle Ray stopped by the house early so Kate could go with him to the nearby courthouse to pick up J.T.

who had been driven there for his official release.

"Good luck," Kate's grandmother said as she stood in the doorway beside Kate's silent mother, their arms linked. Had Grandma forced her mother into the doorway?

"You ready, Kate?" Uncle Ray asked, settling his Nationals baseball cap back on his head. He didn't always wear that hat, and Kate wondered briefly if it was to get a rise out of J.T., who was an Orioles fan.

"Yes—oh, no! Wait a minute!" Kate exclaimed, suddenly remembering. She dashed back upstairs and grabbed a paper bag of clothes for J.T. from the top of her desk so he wouldn't have to wear his prison uniform home. The outfit included J.T.'s T-shirt that said KEEP CALM AND REBOOT, which Kate thought was incredibly appropriate, a pair of his favorite jean shorts, some white ankle-high socks, and old sneakers. Sitting beside her uncle in the truck, Kate clutched the bag of clothes on her lap and prayed silently all the way to town that her brother would still be the same inside.

Despite the late May heat, it was almost cold in the courtroom because of the air-conditioning. Uncle Ray took off his hat, and the two of them chose seats toward the back. When J.T. walked into the courtroom, Kate gasped. It was still a shock to see her brother's hair buzzed off. His hair was so short she could see the shape of his skull. He seemed thinner, too, if that was possible. And even with the air-conditioning on, he was dressed way too warmly in boots, long blue pants, and a sweatshirt that hung on his lanky frame. Still, Kate ached with happiness that her brother was finally coming home. She was doubly glad she'd brought those clothes for him, even if she did have to surrender them to a deputy, who promised to give them to J.T. after his court appearance.

The judge, the master of the court, cleared her throat. "All right, then. We have here Jeremy Tyler," she began, opening a folder on her big desk.

Kate leaned forward, struggling to hear, and turned to her uncle with a puzzled look.

"It's all just protocol," he whispered.

Kate rubbed her arms to get warm and made a mental note to look up that word, *protocol*, later.

There was one order Kate heard clearly and that was when the judge sternly reminded J.T. that the state retained legal custody of him until he was twenty-one.

"If you get into any trouble whatsoever, we can send you right back," she warned. "Do you understand me, Jeremy?"

"Yes, your honor," he replied.

After J.T.'s case was over, Kate and her uncle waited outside the courtroom in the hallway. When a *clanging* noise startled them, they turned to see J.T. coming out of the nearby men's room in the shorts and T-shirt. Kate smiled, figuring the prison uniform had been chucked into the metal trash can, which was fine with her.

Her brother had a funny grin and a soft twinkle in his familiar brown eyes, but his joy was mostly silent. After setting down a lumpy, black plastic bag full of his belongings, he gave his sister a hug, although not the crazy big one she had imagined.

When he stepped away to embrace Uncle Ray, Kate saw

it: the electronic ankle bracelet, a short black leather belt wrapped around J.T.'s ankle with a little box attached. While it wasn't a complete shock—he'd worn one before his trial last summer—it bothered Kate to see it again. Maybe because it was a reminder that J.T. was still perceived as some sort of a criminal. Back at the house, a unit was already connected to the telephone line so it could communicate with the ankle bracelet and monitor J.T.'s movements, twenty-four hours a day. He'd be allowed to go to doctor appointments and meetings with his probation officer, but only certain times that were cleared ahead of time. If he didn't "honor" the perimeter, an alarm would go off, and the police would come.

J.T. saw Kate staring at his ankle.

"Just for two months," he said.

She propped up another smile. At least it would be gone before school started.

A woman approached with paperwork in her hands. "Hi there, Jeremy," she said, extending her hand to J.T. "I'm Miss Hatcher. I'll be your PO."

Right away Kate liked Miss Hatcher because she said "PO" instead of "probation officer." It didn't sound so official—or so mean.

"Is this your family?" Miss Hatcher asked.

"It is," J.T. said. "This is my uncle, Mr. Ray Tyler, and my sister Kate."

Miss Hatcher shook hands with them. Then she turned back to J.T. "Welcome home," she said. "I'll be out to your farm tomorrow morning to see you, and we'll have us a talk, okay?"

Kate watched J.T. swallow and nod. She knew he was nervous. Maybe tomorrow, when he and Miss Hatcher had their talk, he could ask her to call him J.T. and not Jeremy. Maybe that would help a little.

J.T. picked up the black garbage bag.

Uncle Ray said, "Thank you kindly, ma'am."

When his uncle put his baseball cap on, J.T. noticed and said, "What? You think the Nationals have a chance this year?"

"Darn right I do," Uncle Ray said. "It's a new year, a whole new ball game."

J.T. started to smile, and Kate beamed. *A whole new ball game.* She liked that phrase. Uncle Ray put one arm around J.T.'s shoulders and his other arm around Kate, and they headed for the door.

Kate wrote in her journal that night.

We three squished into the front seat of Uncle Ray's truck. It was a long ride home for such a short distance. Uncle Ray doesn't have AC, and it was raining, so maybe the heat and humidity tamped us down. Plus those windshield wipers thumping made a lot of noise. Uncle Ray would ask a simple question, like "How you feelin'?" or me, "Are you hungry?" and J.T. would just mumble a quick answer like "okay" or "not really." Then we'd hear those windshield wipers thump back and forth again.

Pausing with her pen poised over the journal page, Kate looked back at a word she'd just used—*tamped*, a recent vocabulary word. She knew it meant "to pack or push something down, especially by tapping it repeatedly." Which was exactly how she felt. All those weeks of joyous anticipation and crossing the days off on her panda calendar had collided with a cold courtroom where she couldn't hear the judge and had to endure the sight of her brother, thinner than ever, with his hair buzzed off and an electronic bracelet on his ankle. It was no wonder he was so quiet. It was like it was all supposed to be over, but it wasn't. *The windshield wipers thumping* . . . Not by a long shot.

When they arrived home, Kate's grandmother was waiting on the porch with her hands on her cheeks and tears in her eyes. Kerry rushed down the front steps and plowed into J.T., wrapping her skinny little arms around him while Tucker went crazy barking and jumping up and down. Seeing Kerry and his dog, J.T. fully smiled for the first time. He buried his face in Tucker's fur and let the dog practically lick his face off.

Inside the house, Kate's mother stood stiffly in the living room with a plate of warm brownies in her hands. When she didn't say anything, Grandma took the plate from her hands. "Extra chocolate chips and *no nuts!*" she announced cheerfully. Everyone knew that was the way J.T. liked his brownies. Kate thought surely that would prompt a small "welcome home" from her mother, but no such luck. The plate was passed around, but it turned out that, just then, no one was hungry for brownies.

"I've gotta get back. Take care, Angela," Uncle Ray said to Kate's mother. To Grandma, he said, "Good to see you again, Sarah."

It was always funny to hear someone call her grandmother Sarah, or Mrs. Gunter, Kate thought.

Uncle Ray turned to J.T. "Good to have you home, son. I'll see you tomorrow."

At dinner, J.T.'s favorite meal was put on the table: spaghetti, a green salad, and a loaf of hot, buttered garlic bread. Grandma said grace, thanking the lord for J.T.'s safe arrival home, and as soon as she finished, Kate watched her brother wind up a big ball of spaghetti on his fork.

"You don't know how good this tastes," he said around a mouthful.

Kate spooned sauce over her pasta, carefully avoiding the lumps of meat.

"Was the food not very good at that place?" Grandma asked.

J.T. shrugged and swallowed. "It wasn't that bad," he said, "But nowhere near as good as Mom's cooking."

Even though Grandma was the one who made the sauce, no one pointed it out. Instead, they all turned to look at Kate's mother, who sat quietly, picking at her food as if she hadn't even heard the compliment. The air felt heavy. There was an open wound in her family, Kate thought. When was somebody going to make it better?

"Mommy, how come you don't talk to J.T.?" Kerry asked. It took a six-year-old to do it. "Aren't you glad he's home?"

Kate's mother lifted her head to look at J.T. "You never wrote to us."

J.T. met his mother's eyes. "No. I didn't think you wanted me to."

"You weren't here at the end, when your father got so sick."

Just then, the cat, the bell on its collar jingling, jumped off the extra chair at the table, as though sensing the tension, and ran from the room.

J.T. put his fork down. "I don't know what you want me to

say, Mom. I'm sorry for what happened. I'm sorry Dad died and I wasn't here. I am sorry for everything. You think I'm not ashamed of it?"

This was her mother's chance, Kate thought. If only she would say "I understand" or "Let's start over." But she didn't. She just sat there, silent as a stone, with a pained expression, like she didn't know what to do or say.

Kerry's little voice broke the silence again. "Well, I'm glad you're home," she told J.T. "So is Tucker. And so is Jingles!"

"Me too," Kate added.

"We're all glad you're home, dear," Grandma said. She reached across the table to touch both J.T.'s and Mom's hands at the same time. "Angela, please. It's time to forgive. It is time to move forward."

Kate's mother looked up again. Her eyes glistened and then closed. "I am trying."

Another heavy, dead silence followed. Kate wished her mother would try a little harder and say something. But this was how it was now. She knew her mother wasn't well, but it wasn't the kind of sickness you could cure with antibiotics or a week of rest. Something inside her mother was broken.

"It's okay," J.T. said. Then he asked for the bread basket, which got everybody moving forward again.

The bigger disappointment came after dinner, when J.T. wanted to go to bed early and Kate's grandmother had to fetch the key to unlock his room. Kerry followed, and so did Kate, bracing herself because she knew the bed had never been made.

"I had no idea!" Grandma gasped, scooping up dirty socks

from the floor and sending Kate to retrieve fresh sheets. "Give us five minutes," she told J.T.

He went to sit on the stairs.

Kerry, cradling the docile black cat in her arms like a baby, went to sit beside him. "Do you want to hold Jingles?" she asked.

"Five minutes!" Grandma called out to him again while she and Kate hurriedly tucked the bottom sheet around the mattress corners. "We'll have this place fixed up in a jiffy!"

Kate glanced out the door, but all she could see was J.T.'s back, hunched over, unmoving.

~4~

UNSPOKEN

In the morning, Kate's phone woke her with the ding of an arriving text. She reached out from the covers to grab her phone from the night table.

Jess: *You up? Mom's taking me to the mall. Sunglasses and a new bathing suit. Want to come? We can get pedicures! She'll pay!*

Kate hesitated. She and Jess had talked about getting new bathing suits together. Would Jess go without her? Just like that? Kate sat up so she could text back with both hands.

Kate: *JT's first day home.*

She set the phone down and rubbed the sleep from her eyes. Should she ask Jess to hold off on buying the suit? They hadn't even decided one piece or two. And Jess was going to help Kate find some of that lotion that gave you an instant tan. Why couldn't she just wait?

Jess: *Is JT okay?*

Kate picked up her phone. She wasn't going to get into what had happened yesterday.

Kate: *Fine.*

Jess: *Sure you don't want to come?*

Kate was imagining the pedicure. She and Jess and two other friends had gotten pedicures for Jess's eleventh birthday, and Kate had enjoyed the trip to the salon, picking out the color, getting the foot massage, seeing her toes transformed. Reluctantly, she texted back.

Kate: *I should stay home.*

Jess: ☹

Kate: *Sorry*

Jess: *ttyl*

Downstairs, everyone else was already up. J.T. was even dressed and handing his mother a note at the breakfast table.

"I wrote down all the things Uncle Ray did for us. I can take over now," he said.

As she passed by, Kate peered over her mother's shoulder at the list:

CULLING

CHECK THE FEED

CLEAN THE STANDPIPES . . .

"Thank you," Mom said softly.

J.T. put on his baseball cap, giving it a tug front and back, and said, "Uncle Ray won't need to come anymore. I know he's here this morning to mow, but I told him I could learn how to do that, too."

Suddenly, Kate felt hopeful. Quickly, she ate a bowl of cereal and got dressed so she could follow J.T. outside.

"Gassing up for Uncle Ray," he said when Kate approached the pump down by the tractor sheds where he was standing.

Kate smiled. "I'm glad you're home."

"Me too. You have no idea."

She waited for him to hang up the nozzle and cap the tractor's fuel tank.

"Sorry about Mom," she said, eager to talk. "I mean, the way she is now."

J.T. wiped his hands on a rag he pulled from under the tractor seat. "It has a name, you know. What Mom's got."

"You mean why she won't leave the house?"

"Yeah. She has agoraphobia," J.T. said. "She's afraid of having another panic attack in public, so she doesn't want to go anywhere. She only feels safe in the house. I talked to Miss Laurie, my counselor at Cliffside, about it."

"I didn't know it had a name," Kate said. "I know she takes medicine."

J.T. caught his sister's eyes. "We have to help her, Kate. Grandma can't keep coming up here all the way from North Carolina. She's got a life with Grandpa. He needs her, too. I know that Mom is their only child, but we can't expect Grandma to give up her life for us."

Kate's lips remained parted. Her brother's compassion was unbelievable.

"Wait!" she said when he started walking away. It had been nine long months since they'd had a conversation, and there was a lot she wanted to talk about. "I wanted to tell you that I got an e-mail from Brady on my birthday."

"No!" J.T. snapped, stopping abruptly and whirling around.

"Do *not* be mentioning Brady to me—or Digger either! Do you hear?"

Surprised, Kate drew back.

"Sorry," J.T. said quickly, lowering his voice. "I didn't mean to yell. And I'm sorry I didn't write to you." He lifted his hands and then let them drop. "I didn't know what to say."

"You could've just told me what you did," Kate suggested gently, recalling how desperate she'd been for even the tiniest bit of information. She lifted her shoulders. "Like what you had for breakfast—"

"But I didn't want to talk about it," J.T. said, cutting her off. "I *still* don't, so just let it go, okay?"

"Okay," Kate instantly agreed. But she couldn't help herself. When he walked away, she trotted after him. "Can I tell you something I did? That Mom doesn't know?"

"What? About sending the trumpet?" J.T. asked, smacking at a deerfly on his arm while he kept moving. "I knew you did it behind Mom's back."

"You did?" Kate was surprised.

"Of course I knew."

But how? Kate wondered, slowing down. And why hadn't he thanked her?

"Well, that's not it!" she called after him.

J.T. kept going.

"I became a vegetarian," Kate declared when she caught up to him.

Her brother finally stopped and stared at her. "What?"

Kate nodded vigorously. "Yeah. I don't eat meat."

"Why?"

"I saw a film, J.T. It showed how they slaughter animals—
how *awful* it is. Not just the chickens, but the cows and the
pigs—and the lambs. I cried so hard. I swore I'd never eat meat
again. I wish no one would eat meat."

Her brother's face softened. "Kate," he said, opening his
hands. "You *live* on a chicken farm!"

"I know." Kate screwed up her face. "*I know!*"

"Mom hasn't noticed?"

She shook her head. "Grandma hasn't either. Jess is the only
one I told."

"Are you getting protein and stuff?"

"Sure, it's not a problem. I researched it. I eat a lot of peanut butter and beans. It's easy, 'cause I'm the one who does the
food shopping *and* most of the cooking when Grandma's not
here. Did you know that? Every other month, she goes home
to North Carolina. I go to the grocery store with Jess's mom. I
take the bags and everything."

J.T. stared at her. "You didn't tell me that."

"It's hard sometimes," Kate went on, glad to have a sympa-
thetic ear. "Like when we drop Jess off for a piano lesson on our
way to the Food Lion. Nobody else I know has a mother who
won't drive."

"How do you know what to cook?" J.T. asked, apparently still
stuck on the fact that Kate was preparing entire meals now.

Kate raised her eyebrows. "Grandma and I wrote up dinners
on index cards. Every meal has a protein, a starch, and a vege-
table. The cards are in a rubber band on top of the bread box, if
you want to see."

J.T. frowned and rubbed his chin.

"Don't tell Mom I'm not eating meat, okay?" Kate pleaded. "Don't tell Grandma either."

"I won't," he said, hesitating. "Look, Miss Hatcher's coming any minute. I need to be out front."

On the porch steps, they sat side by side, staring down the long driveway. The sun felt good on Kate's face. They had shared a secret. They could talk now, she thought. The hopeful feeling was coming back.

"Are you looking forward to school?" Kate asked gingerly.

Her brother shrugged. "I'm glad I'm not at Cliffside anymore," he said. "But I don't know about school."

Most kids hadn't seen J.T. in more than a year, and while everyone knew he'd been sent to a juvenile detention center, Kate hoped no one would hold what he did against him or say mean things, especially since J.T. had been bullied in middle school. A boy named Curtis Jenkins used to call him Chicken Man. Curtis had stuffed chicken feathers into J.T.'s locker and once accused him out loud of stinking up the classroom by not cleaning the chicken manure out of his shoes (only he didn't call it manure).

"Guess I worry about it," he added.

Kate nodded softly in agreement. "Me too." She didn't have much faith that the anti-bullying campaign in middle school had sunk in deep enough to carry over into high school. It was a nice effort, for sure. A "Words that Hurt" program took up an entire afternoon with students acting out roles on the stage in the auditorium. The students designed T-shirts and crafted posters. Kate and Jess made one together: DON'T STAND BY— STAND UP! But Kate felt flat about the anti-bullying stuff now. She suspected that for a lot of kids it was all a halfhearted gesture, like the fire drill or the canned food they brought in at Thanksgiving. Just something you had to do at school that day.

She shifted her position on the steps to face her brother. "You should try out for marching band," she said brightly.

"Why?" J.T. asked.

"Because you play the trumpet!"

When J.T. didn't respond, Kate tried again. "Band camp's in August, and maybe you'd get to know a few kids before school started."

Pressing the tips of his long fingers together, J.T. looked down. "I don't ever want to touch that trumpet again."

Kate just stared at him like, *what in the heck does that mean?* She didn't get it.

But J.T. got up and walked off across the yard, because Miss Hatcher had just turned up the driveway.

It wasn't going to be easy, Kate was realizing. And while she didn't want to admit it so soon, she knew her brother was different now. You couldn't talk about Cliffside with him. And you couldn't mention Brady and Digger. Both of which Kate could understand. But the trumpet? Why would J.T. not play it anymore and refuse to join the marching band? It just didn't make sense.

By noon, Miss Hatcher had left, and Uncle Ray had finished the mowing and turned off the tractor. In the quiet that followed, Tucker stretched out, his dog tags clinking on the wooden porch floor, while Kate lay on the porch swing, pushing herself back and forth with one foot. An open book lay on her chest, but her eyes were closed as she wondered if Jess had found her bathing suit and whether she and her mother also got lunch at the mall. Maybe even sweet potato fries in the food court. Jess and Kate always got a batch and split them. Sometimes, it was all they ate.

"Uncle Ray, what you got there?"

The sound of J.T.'s voice prompted Tucker to scramble and dash from the porch. Kate held the book and sat up. She could see that, down at the tractor shed, J.T. and Uncle Ray had something in their hands.

"What is it?" she asked, after running to where they stood.

In the sweaty T-shirt he'd taken off, her uncle held a sorrowful sight: three dead baby bunnies, their little bodies mangled and bloodied. He didn't need to explain it. The mower blade had hit their nest. It had happened before. Kate winced and started to look away but saw that J.T. held something, too. A single survivor, a tiny brown cottontail missing one leg, was cradled in the palm of his hand.

"What are you going to do with him?" Kate asked.

"Best thing to do, Kate, is just put him out of his misery," Uncle Ray said. "I'm so sorry. I told J.T. I'd take care of it."

"No!" Kate protested. "Can't we help him? I'll do it! I'll take care of him!"

Her uncle hesitated and looked from Kate to J.T. "What do you think?"

J.T. met Kate's eyes.

"Please," Kate begged again.

Her brother turned to Uncle Ray and shrugged. "I say let her try. Let her find out how much work it is to raise a baby rabbit, let alone one without a leg!"

"You'll have to dab ointment on that stump, Kate, to keep

away infection. And this little, you'll have to feed it several times a day," Uncle Ray warned. "We'll have to get special formula at the feed store, and even then there's no guarantee."

"I understand," she said, pressing her hands together. "Really!"

Within the hour, Kate had a baby bunny, encased in a fuzzy sock and snug in her hand, accepting droplets of warm formula from a plastic syringe. She'd already texted Jess twice to come see him as soon as she got back.

"Will he live?" Kerry asked, sitting tight against Kate on the living room couch. On her lap she held the baby bunny's new home: a flannel-lined shoebox.

"Don't know," Kate said. "I hope so."

"I promise I'll keep Jingles away," Kerry said.

Just then Kate's cell phone alerted her to a message. It was from Jess, but no response about the bunny. No words at all. Just a picture of a bathing suit on a dressing room bench. The suit was dark blue. Two piece.

"Someday this bunny and Jingles can be friends," Kerry said.

"He'll be hopping around one day, you wait and see," J.T. said, surprising the girls that he stood behind them.

Kerry's face lit up. "We should name him Hoppy!"

"Hoppy," Kate repeated, trying to get back into the moment. "Perfect!"

The baby bunny and J.T.'s arrival home truly marked the beginning of summer. Soon, the pink and white crepe myrtle trees blossomed as though loving the longer, hotter days. The cicadas got louder, making the air hum with their noise. And a different kind of routine settled in. J.T. was the first one up every day, until one morning when Kate's mother beat him to the kitchen and had bacon frying. The good smell got everyone up early. "You need something more than cereal if you're going to go out and work all morning," Kate heard Mom tell J.T.

Every morning Kate had chores, dishes, or vacuuming, then she was free to write in her journal or read or do whatever she wanted. She fed the baby bunny every three hours, even setting her phone alarm at night, and kept antibiotic cream on the missing back leg's stump. Some afternoons, she babysat her three little girl cousins—Alice, Annie, and Alyssa. Kate had reconnected with Jess, and the girls had agreed that half the money they made babysitting over the summer would go toward the hefty admission fee to an animal sanctuary in North Carolina where they could actually hold a baby tiger on their laps. They would ride down next summer and stay with Kate's grandparents so there wouldn't be travel expenses. On sleepovers, the girls also started compiling a list of wildlife rehab centers they could apply to for volunteer work when they were older. So far, they'd found a koala refuge in Australia and an elephant foundation in Thailand that captivated them with an online video of a young woman giving a baby elephant a sudsy bath in the river.

Grandma had chosen to stay on over the summer, and despite what J.T. had said about her other life, Kate was grateful. Her grandmother had taken over the cooking and braiding Kerry's long hair. She was even carpooling with Jess's mom to the middle school for the girls' field hockey camp one week, and the next, into town for a pottery class. It was during this week that Kate's mother surprised everyone by offering to feed the baby bunny while Kate was away.

"This is how I hold him," Kate said, adjusting the fuzzy sock. Her fingers touched her mother's as she handed over the tiny rabbit.

"I think I've got it," her mother said. "Oh, my. So tiny. So hungry!" Her mouth turned up at the corners, and when their eyes met, Kate smiled back.

Occasionally, there were trips to the Tastee-Freez for soft ice cream and on really hot days—if there weren't many jellyfish—swimming in the river. Since his ankle bracelet was waterproof and the river was practically in their backyard, even J.T. joined the girls for a swim one afternoon.

"Cannonball!" he shouted before jumping in off a fallen locust tree that jutted over the water and making a huge splash.

The girls got soaked, their screams turning to laughter as they got their hands ready to spray J.T. when he surfaced.

But he didn't come up.

Slowly, the smile melted off Kate's face. Treading water, she turned to Jess.

"Oh, my God," Jess said.

Suddenly, J.T. emerged from the dark, cool water, relieving both girls, but then startling them, too, with the stricken look on his face. He wiped the water out of his eyes and hauled out of the river fast, slipping once on the slick, grassy bank before grabbing his towel and heading back up the path.

"What's wrong?" Kate called after him.

Jess slapped the water and hollered, "J.T., come back!"

When he didn't even turn around, Kate guessed that maybe

J.T. had been thinking about a little boy who died from exposure in the same river just over a year ago. Judging from her rueful expression, Jess may have thought the same thing, too. But the girls didn't talk about it. Despite their friendship, a lot of things went unspoken between them. They never talked about how Kate's mother had changed or the stigma from J.T.'s crime that hung over the Tyler family, or how embarrassing it was for Kate to go food shopping with Jess's mom. Kate was never sure why they didn't talk about these things, although she did worry she'd lose Jess if there were too many problems. In life, she was learning, there were some things you just didn't talk about.

The rest of summer slid by quickly. While the girls had their fun, it seemed that all J.T. did was work. He weeded and watered the gardens, mowed the yard, painted the shed roofs, and took care of the chickens, which was huge because every day he had to remove the dead ones and then do the culling. To Kate, this was the absolute worst job in the entire world. Culling meant picking out the weakened chicks, or the ones not growing as fast, and getting rid of them. It seemed like culling was playing God, deciding who would live and who would die, and she didn't want any part of it.

Maybe, Kate thought, hard work was J.T.'s way of trying to redeem himself and make up for what he'd done. He didn't even watch TV or go on his computer much.

By mid-August, J.T.'s dark hair had grown back in and the ankle bracelet was gone. Kate's bunny had grown big enough to need a wire cage and had to be moved outside. He was getting around just fine on three legs, but still, Kate kept lots of hay and even a small piece of old carpeting in his cage so he had something soft to hop on. Jess wanted Kate to go shopping for school clothes at the mall in Annapolis, but everything was more expensive there, and Kate had to tell her she couldn't go. Instead, Grandma took all three of the kids to the Walmart in Easton for clothes and school supplies. J.T. didn't have to check in with his probation officer as often, so no one worried when it all took longer than they'd planned, and they decided to stop for pizza on the way home. They all laughed when Kerry said, "I want juth," and had to repeat herself three times before anyone could figure out she meant "juice." Even Kerry giggled, flashing her missing-front-teeth smile.

Only one person wasn't there. Kate quickly texted her mother as their meal arrived: *We'll bring pizza home, so you don't have to cook.*

New school clothes. Dinner out. Laughter. Under the table, Kate tapped her hands together and was quietly grateful. This was how her life used to be. This was how it was supposed to be. It had a name, too: *normal*. And normal had never felt so good, Kate thought while carefully picking the pepperoni off her slice of pizza.

But then came the first day of school.

~5~

FAR FROM HEAVENLY

We have a lot to cover this year. So be forewarned. This class is *not* a social hour!" Kate's new English teacher, Mrs. Langley, looked up from her notes and flashed a threatening look at the class over her reading glasses.

Kate was listening. She wanted to work hard. She *had* to do well. Ever since she'd started going to public school, bringing home a good report card was about the only thing that made her mother even a little bit proud of her. "Straight A's," her mother might actually say with the glimmer of a smile and her eyes connecting with Kate's. "Good job." And yet Kate was distracted and anxious, because the first day of high school was not what she had envisioned.

The shoes were the first clue. Kate should have paid more attention. All those niggling doubts about the way she looked came flooding back. She had read the dress code on the website. It said "no flip-flops, no slippers, and no bare feet." So she figured sneakers would be okay. They were new—plain white, comfy, and inexpensive. Grandma was delighted she'd found such a great deal. Kate hadn't thought much about them until a girl on the bus made a weird face. "Off brand," she heard the girl say before she and her friend grunted and laughed behind their hands.

But it was true. No one was wearing sneakers like hers—none of the girls, anyway. Most of them—including Jess—were wearing flip-flops!

During second class, Honors English, Kate was still beating herself up over it. She had wanted this day to be perfect. Why hadn't she talked to Jess about this? Why hadn't Jess *said* something? Was it because Kate hadn't gone shopping with her?

"Each and every student in this room needs to come prepared—be on time and ready to work." Mrs. Langley continued.

It didn't help that Kate's heart was still pounding from the run to class either. She'd gotten lost in the upstairs hallway and had almost been late. Somehow she'd had the wrong room number in her head—and it was a long way from 213 to 109!

Nervous, Kate twisted several strands of her shoulder-length hair with her index finger and thumb. It wasn't just the shoes either. She should have done something with her hair, too. She should have straightened it. But she hated the flat iron because she was always burning herself on it. Plus it took too long. She should have made a ponytail. Anything would have been better than nothing.

Tucking her hair behind one ear, Kate scanned the handout, her eyes lighting on the book list. She recognized some of the titles like *To Kill a Mockingbird*, *The Scarlet Letter*, *Romeo and Juliet*. But others were new to her and had interesting titles like *I Know Why the Caged Bird Sings* by Maya Angelou. She was going to love the reading.

"Cell phones and iPods are a distraction in class. They are *not allowed*! All of your electronic devices should be in your locker during the day." Mrs. Langley's voice hammered out the warning: "Rest assured, people, that I will confiscate these devices if I see them being used!"

Kate glanced at the girl across the aisle and recognized Glenda Newbie from eighth grade. Glenda looked really tan. But Kate wondered why she'd put on so much black eyeliner. Other than lip gloss, Kate still didn't use any makeup. Like Jess, she believed true beauty was natural, not something fake you painted on your face. When they made eye contact, Kate started to smile and widen her eyes, as in, *Can you believe this teacher?* But Glenda swung her head around and turned away as she shook back her long, straight-as-a-broom blond hair.

In fact, the eye makeup made Glenda Newbie look like a raccoon, Kate decided.

From the corner of her eyes, Kate watched Glenda cross her legs. Glenda had on cute leather sandals and what appeared to be fresh black nail polish that made her toes look bruised.

Kate pulled in her sneakered feet. What a dork she must look like in her *off-brand* sneakers, her loose-fitting jeans, and her plain pink T-shirt that hung on her lean frame. Next time she did the wash, she would throw everything in the dryer for an extra ten minutes to see if they'd shrink.

Or not! Why should she? Just because most girls wore snug tops and short skirts didn't mean she had to do it, too.

Did it?

Confused, and suddenly panicked, Kate stared down at the syllabus in her hands. She gritted her teeth. There was so much for her to get used to—the clothes, the makeup, the way older kids acted, the block schedule with ninety minutes per class, which seemed so long. It was a huge mistake for her to be in high school, wasn't it? She was only thirteen. She should have been in the eighth grade, not the ninth! The year she had skipped back in fifth grade when she entered public school had messed her up now!

"You need to listen. You need to participate," Mrs. Langley told them.

Listen . . . participate . . . Kate blinked and bit a fingernail and tried to focus, but already her mind was straying again. She couldn't help it. She had imagined the first day of high school so many times over the summer—it almost glittered like a distant star in her mind. New classes, new friends—a new beginning! It had been almost a year since her father had died. J.T. had been home for three months. It was way past time for a new start. But the first day was here, and it was far from the heavenly new chapter in her life that she had imagined for herself—or for her brother, because no one had sat with him on the bus that morning.

"Number eight!" Mrs. Langley called out as she tossed something into the wastebasket that made a heavy thud. "No food and drink allowed in this room!"

Number eight? Kate licked her lips and glanced around. She

must have spaced out again. She did not want to start out this way, not listening. She swallowed hard and stretched her eyes.

Mrs. Langley continued: "Cheating. *Suspected* cheating. Or *attempted* cheating will result in a zero on the assignment and disciplinary action. . . ."

Kate frowned. Why would a teacher have to even say this?

When a buzzer finally sounded, Kate was glad. She and the others in her class gathered their books and notebooks. Pens clicked. Backpacks were scooped up from the floor and sweatshirts whipped off the backs of chairs.

Kate fled down the hallway quickly, quietly, avoiding eyes by looking down. Of course, this way, she couldn't help but notice everyone's feet and the fact that most girls did not have sneakers on. She did, however, see one girl wearing a pair of bright green Crocs and another with socks and sandals. That had to be worse than plain old off-brand sneakers, didn't it? *Who decided these things?*

She hurried because it was a long walk from her English class to the cafeteria. She and Jess had the same lunch period, and they had arranged to meet outside the girls' room closest to the cafeteria before going in. She'd talk to Jess about the shoe thing then.

But Jess was waiting with a new girl named Olivia, and the three of them had to rush to get in a long line for hot lunch.

"Olivia moved here last month from Catonsville," Jess said.

"Welcome," Kate responded, trying to be friendly, but wishing she could have had some time alone with Jess. "Where's Catonsville?"

"Up near Baltimore," Olivia said. "Not that far."

Olivia seemed like a nice girl. She was a little bit heavyset and had long black hair that she'd pulled back into a French braid. She also wore beige flats with tiny gold-colored studs on them and, Kate couldn't help but notice, thick violet mascara that made her eyelashes look heavy.

"We're in Latin and US history together," Jess said.

Kate was a little jealous. She was going to miss being with Jess. They had only one class together, and that was geometry.

"You should see the homework we already have," Jess went on. "Hey!" She turned to Kate. "Olivia played field hockey last year at her middle school. Do you think Coach Dietrich would let her join the team late?"

Kate shrugged. "I don't know." Why was Jess so gung ho about Olivia, whom she had just met?

Hot lunch didn't look so great. Some kind of macaroni with tomato sauce and *ground beef* on it. At least, Kate thought, there was a tiny green salad and a roll with butter. By the time they filled their trays and found a seat, however, there wasn't much time left to eat anything anyway—never mind talk about shoes.

"Hey, I see J.T.," said Jess, who was sitting directly across the table from Kate.

At first, Kate acted like she didn't hear. On top of everything else, she did not want to have to worry about her brother again.

"Kate," Jess repeated, tapping the edge of Kate's tray with her fingers, "I see J.T."

Unable to avoid it any longer, Kate looked up. "Really? Where?"

Jess indicated with her fork, and reluctantly, Kate turned to see. Just as she'd feared, J.T. was alone, at a small table with four chairs. The scene tugged at her heart. She wondered if she should get up and go sit with him.

"That's your brother?" Olivia asked.

Kate didn't respond. The cafeteria was jammed with kids, some walking around, trays in hand, looking for seats, and yet those three chairs around J.T. remained empty. He was an island in a busy stream.

"What year is he?" Olivia asked.

When Kate didn't answer, Jess did. "He's a sophomore."

Sadly, Kate watched her brother. She had made him a peanut butter sandwich that morning (she should have made one for herself), and he seemed to be eating it quickly. Why wouldn't anyone sit with him? The sight was so painful that when Kate finally turned back to her own lunch, her appetite was gone.

"Oh, no!" Jess suddenly exclaimed, putting a hand to her mouth. Her eyes were fixed in J.T.'s direction.

Whipping around, Kate saw her brother push back from the table and stand up, milk dripping down the front of his shirt.

"Someone tossed a milk carton!" Jess exclaimed.

"Where?" Kate asked, scraping back her chair as she stood to look.

"Over there!" Jess stood up and pointed. "It's Curtis Jenkins!"

Kate saw how Curtis and two other boys were whooping it up with laughter. Kate recognized one of the others as a boy named Hooper.

She felt her heart drop. It was happening, she thought. It was happening all over again.

Grabbing her backpack, Kate started pushing between the

chairs to get to J.T., but then the buzzer rang and everyone else got up to go, trapping her.

"Kate!" Jess called from across the table to her.

She needed to get to her brother right away.

"Kate, wait!" Jess called again.

"What's happening?" Olivia asked. "What's with her brother?"

But Kate shoved her way through the crowd and didn't stick around to hear how Jess would explain it all to her new friend.

~6~
NO BIG DEAL

"A re you okay?" Kate asked breathlessly. She used a Kleenex to dab at some of the milk on her brother's shirt.

J.T. brushed her hand away. "Yeah, yeah. I'm okay. Just go on to class, Kate. It's not your problem."

"It is my problem. You're my brother!"

"Yeah, well, if I were you, right now I'd pretend we weren't related."

"Stop it!"

"I'm *serious*. Just go!" J.T. said, wiping his pants with an already saturated napkin.

Kate glanced around, incredulous, as kids rushed past right and left to get to class. Like nothing had happened! Why wasn't a teacher coming to help? Didn't anybody see what had just happened?

"Are you going to the office?" Kate asked.

"What for?" J.T. snapped the question as he threw the wadded napkin on the table.

"What for? What do you mean *what for*? To report those guys! You know who threw it, don't you?"

J.T. glared at her. "No. Who was it?"

"Curtis!" Kate exclaimed. "Jess and I saw him laughing. Curtis and that boy who hung out with him in middle school."

"Hooper Delaney?"

Kate nodded.

"Did you actually *see* one of them throw it?"

Kate still held the soggy tissue. "No."

"Then how are you going to prove it?"

"Tons of people saw!" Kate said. "Jess was sitting across from me. She saw the whole thing!"

J.T. shook his head as he lifted his backpack.

"What are you going to do?" Kate pressed.

"I'm going to the bathroom to clean up." J.T. paused and looked his sister in the eye. "Kate, please, just leave it, okay? It's *my* business, not yours."

Kate felt sick to her stomach as she watched J.T. walk away. She looked to see if Jess had waited for her, but her friend was nowhere to be seen. The cafeteria was practically empty. The buzzer rang again. She would be late for a class on the first day of school.

Fortunately, Kate's next class wasn't too far down the hall from the cafeteria. And, as it turned out, her teacher was late, too. Kate took the first open seat she found, at the front of the room, before Mr. Ellison walked in. After pulling a pen from her purse, she sat back in the chair, still trying to catch her breath.

When Mr. Ellison closed the door, chitchat in the room stopped. He was incredibly tall. Young, too, and good-looking,

Kate thought. Wow. Her most anticipated class was about to begin with a really cool teacher, and she felt like crying because of her brother. Quickly, she glanced around the room, knowing that she would see a mix of upperclassmen. She was one of two freshmen taking Creative Writing. Another syllabus was dropped on her desk. As Mr. Ellison discussed what they would cover—essays, profiles, scene writing—Kate began to relax a little and tune in.

"Later on, we're going to try some vignettes that include plot, setting, and dialogue," Mr. Ellison said, his deep voice upbeat, enthusiastic. He didn't refer to notes as he spoke. "You're also going to keep journals."

This class would be amazing, Kate thought. She had read on the school website that Mr. Ellison was new to Corsica High School. Previously, he'd been a middle school English teacher in Montana. Kate had never been farther west than Toledo, Ohio, where her grandparents once lived. Reading Mr. Ellison's bio on the website, she had pictured snowcapped mountains with snarling cougars and open plains with wild horses running.

"Every day we will begin this class with fifteen minutes of freewriting," Mr. Ellison announced. "I'll give you a prompt. I may write a word on the board or put an object on my desk, and you'll respond by writing continuously for fifteen minutes. The whole idea is to move that pen in your hands and see where you end up."

He pushed aside some papers and sat on the corner of his desk. Kate was surprised, but she liked his informality.

"This will help you get in the habit of writing every day," he said. "Second, it will help you get in the writing *mood*."

Honors English and Creative Writing were going to be her two favorite classes; she could feel it already.

"Let's start right now," Mr. Ellison said. "Take out your journals. If you don't have one, raise your hand, and I'll give you a piece of paper. Write about what you're thinking right now. What do you expect from this class?"

Kate rummaged through her backpack and took out the notebook she had carefully chosen as her journal for Creative Writing class. It was identical to the one in which she'd written all summer. She liked that notebook. It had a dark blue cover, narrow lines on the pages, and three cardboard inserts that divided the notebook into sections. Each insert had a pocket that Kate imagined using for ideas she had jotted down on colored index cards.

"Everyone—*please*—begin," Mr. Ellison said. "I'm not going to collect and read these journals. Just relax and write whatever comes into your head."

Kate began:

I'm going to love this class, because I hope to be a writer. I mean, first of all I want to work with animals somehow, like maybe saving endangered animals. But I want to be a writer, too. I love finding the right word to describe something. Like <u>stoic</u> for my father during his years of kidney dialysis. And <u>indefatigable</u> for my grandmother, who is seventy and never seems to run out of energy. Kate paused.

"Be honest!" Mr. Ellison encouraged them.

It's my brother, Kate began slowly. *It's like a nightmare coming true. At lunch today someone threw a carton of milk . . .*

✱

After school, Kate met up with Jess for junior varsity field hockey practice and was relieved to hear Olivia didn't want to join the team after all. She felt a little guilty thinking this, but now, she figured, she could totally focus on the game. All of the eighth-grade season she'd been the goalie, and she was excited that the high school coach was letting her try out for a different position. Halfback, maybe, where she could actually run and drive the ball. Their first game was coming up in a couple weeks, and Kate hoped she'd be one of the starters in a new position. For nearly two hours, Kate focused only on the drills, driving the ball up the field and whacking it into the goal. Afterward, Jess's mother gave Kate a ride home.

As she walked toward the house, Kate could hear Kerry's singsong voice from inside the house. Her little sister had been so excited about second grade. Was it all she expected? Kate was eager to find out what was for dinner, too, and hoped it was her grandmother's spicy stuffed peppers she smelled.

J.T. sat on the front steps, but stood up when Kate approached. "Don't say anything about what happened today," he told her.

Kate stopped. She didn't want to promise him that she wouldn't tell. She let the backpack slip off her shoulder. Her eyes fell away from his.

"It's *my* business, Kate. It's my thing that I have to sort out."

He was right about that, Kate thought. She locked eyes with her brother. "What are you going to do?"

"I don't know. Hopefully, it's over," he said. Then he emphasized, "I don't want to make a big deal out of it."

Kate hesitated.

"I'm not one of your injured animals, Kate. I can take care of myself."

"All right," she agreed. "I won't say anything. But if it happens again, J.T., will you report it? You can't let him start this in high school."

"I know," he said. "Look, I've got to do the culling before dinner."

Kate watched him walk off, Tucker trotting alongside. He would spend part of the next hour doing the job she hated most.

Just then, Kerry burst through the front door. "Kate! I have homework!"

Kate dropped her things and opened her arms for a hug. "No way!" she said, beaming and kneeling to give her little sister a hug.

The next morning, Kate chose her clothes more carefully. She wore a denim skirt, a striped top, and sandals. She pulled her hair into a ponytail and made a peanut butter sandwich so she didn't have to depend on the hot lunch. On the bus, she sat in the seat Jess saved for her and listened to her friend talk up a storm about how she was going to propose a "Quote of the Day" idea to the first meeting of those interested in working for the in-school TV station.

"I've already got twelve ideas," Jess said.

Kate scanned the quotes in Jess's notebook. "You're going to read these on the morning news?"

Jess arched her eyebrows and nodded enthusiastically.

Kate craned her neck to see if anyone had sat with her brother up front.

"Kate, if you need to sit with him, go ahead," Jess said.

"Actually, I think someone just sat down with him."

"Good! I feel so bad for J.T. 'cause of what happened yesterday in the cafeteria," Jess said. "I prayed about it last night. You know what my first quote on the air will be?"

Warily, Kate shook her head.

"Ephesians 4:32. Be kind and compassionate to one another, forgiving each other—"

"Jess!" Kate interrupted, "You're not going to quote the Bible on the morning announcements, are you?"

"Yes!" she said, eagerly nodding. "Why not?"

"Are you kidding me? They'll tease you for that! You'll be committing social suicide!"

Jess smiled back with self-assurance. "It doesn't matter. I've thought about this, Kate. I want to make a difference."

"Are all your quotes going to come from the Bible?"

Jess started to shrug. "Maybe not all of them."

Kate rolled her eyes. How could Jess be so naïve? "I don't even think you can do this in public school!" she warned.

"Okay, okay. I kind of figured that. But if they say yes, then I will. I mean, why not?"

Kate had to look away. Why indeed? If Jess wanted to quote from the Bible, then she should do it, right? It was who she was, a religious person who had no problem with people knowing it. Kate didn't feel the same, but she hadn't allowed this difference to come between them.

"Look, I just don't want to see you get teased," Kate said. "They'll call you a Jesus freak or something."

"I can't help what they think. It's who I am, Kate."

Kate didn't say anymore. She didn't think the school would allow Bible quotes on the morning news anyway, so it probably wouldn't be an issue.

When the bus stopped at school, Kate bid good-bye to Jess and rushed to catch up with her brother. "Hey!" she said, touching his elbow. "Someone sat with you this morning!"

J.T. kept walking. "Oh, wow."

"Come on, you know what I mean. It's a start. I think things will be okay."

"Yeah."

Kate stayed by her brother's side until they were inside the front doors. J.T.'s locker was off to the right while Kate's was to the left.

"Good luck today," she said softly before they separated.

"Thanks," J.T. mumbled.

But both were stopped by a jarring sight: a banner made of loose-leaf notebook paper that had been taped over a long string hung across the hallway near J.T.'s locker. Large letters in thick black marker read:

THE CHICKEN MAN RETURNS

~7~
COWARDS

A hush fell over the crowded hallway. The chatter, the stream of laughter, the slamming of locker doors—all of it stopped. Kids stepped back to clear a path and watched as Kate and J.T. slowly moved forward.

It was like falling into a trance, Kate thought, a trance of disbelief. She kept thinking that as she got closer, the individual letters would clarify and become something different, or else disappear. Only they didn't. Instead, the letters seemed to grow larger—and more menacing.

THE CHICKEN MAN RETURNS

Kate's mouth went dry. Her heart pounded.

J.T. stood silent beside her.

"Who did this?" Kate asked softly, even though she'd suspected right away it was Curtis. It wasn't like her to make a scene, but shock was quickly turning to anger. "Who did this?"

she repeated, her trembling voice a little louder.

Looking around, Kate saw some of the kids shake their heads and shrug. She also heard some giggling and caught a few smirks. But no one said anything.

J.T. remained silent and seemed stunned.

"*Somebody* saw!" Kate declared, her voice so loud it surprised even herself. "Who was it?"

"Come on, Kate," J.T. said, putting his hand on her arm.

But Kate pulled away and stared at the gawking students. And in that moment, she had a crystallized flashback to middle school, the day all of eighth grade sat in the library during Anti-Bullying Week watching the assistant principal draw a diagram on the board. In the middle, he drew a small circle and called it the Victim. In a semicircle around the Victim, other circles appeared: the Students Who Bullied, the Followers, the Passive Bullies, the Disengaged Onlookers, and the Possible Defenders. They were in that circle right now, weren't they? Everyone standing there knew it. How could they not care? Did they think it was *funny*?

Don't stand by—stand up.

But not a single person did.

"You're all a bunch of cowards!" Kate blurted out, on the verge of tears.

"Kate, please." J.T. grabbed her arm and tried to lead her away, but Kate wriggled out of his grasp.

"You're going to make it worse!" he whispered harshly.

Kate ignored the warning. She dropped her backpack on the floor and marched over to where the banner was attached at one end with adhesive tape to the wall. The crowd parted to let her through, and everyone watched as Kate reached up to rip off the tape. She walked to the other side of the hall, the banner trailing on the floor behind her, and ripped the other end off. Quickly, noisily, she gathered the papers in her arms, squashing them against her chest, and retrieved her backpack. She looked for J.T., but he was gone.

People started moving. The show was over.

Or was it? Kate spotted Curtis Jenkins in the crowd. He was partially hidden, but stretching his neck to watch her. There was no question it had been him. Kate recognized the long dirty blond hair brushing his eyes, the ever-present camo shirt, the trademark smirk.

She walked up to him. "Was it you, Curtis?"

Kids began stopping to see what would happen next.

Curtis faked innocence and grinned. He pointed to himself. "Who? Me?"

Hooper Delaney called out, "Whoa, Curtis! Shame on you!" Then he bent over laughing.

Curtis threw up his hands. "I didn't have anything to do with it!"

"You're a liar, Curtis!" It was J.T.'s voice from behind Kate.

Curtis puffed up his chest. "Who's calling me a liar?"

"I am," J.T. said without flinching. He was a little bit taller than Curtis, but he didn't have the bully's bulk or his muscular arms.

Curtis lifted a fist. "Nobody calls me a liar! Especially not you, Chicken Man."

J.T. slipped off his backpack and curled his own two hands into fists.

Kate's mouth dropped. This was like a scene out of a movie! She had never seen J.T. curl his fists at anyone in his entire life! She didn't think he even knew how to fight! When Curtis pulled his arm back to throw a punch, Kate dropped the crumpled banner and jumped between the boys.

"Stop!" she screamed at Curtis before whirling around to face her brother. Lowering her voice, she warned, "J.T., if you fight and get in trouble, they'll send you back!"

"Come on, Chicken Man, you gonna let your little sister save you? You a coward, too? A coward and a killer?"

J.T. lunged forward when he heard that, but Kate blocked him, then spun around and used both hands to knock Curtis back, a feat she accomplished only because she took him by surprise.

A teacher clapped loudly. "What's going on here?"

Curtis ducked and slid away into the crowd. Like a snake, Kate thought.

"Kate, do *not* say anything," J.T. whispered urgently.

The teacher who had clapped stood watching for a few more seconds, then walked back into her classroom.

The crowd cleared out.

"Stay out of it," J.T. warned Kate again as he gathered his stuff. "I can handle this myself." He hoisted his backpack and stalked off.

But Kate was not going to stay out of it. After scooping up the crumpled banner, she grabbed her things and headed toward the school's main office.

When the buzzer sounded for first period, Kate was still standing at the front counter waiting to talk to the school secretary. Again, she would be late for class, this time her first biology class and lab. But what else could she do? Ignore what happened? If she did, it would continue. It would get worse.

There were at least four others waiting for help in front of her. How long would this take? Nervous, Kate bit her lip. She hoped that J.T. had gone on to class so at least *he* wouldn't get into trouble.

Eager to get the report done and return to class, Kate tapped her sandaled foot nervously. While she waited, the girl beside her begged to see the school nurse; "Come on, I'm *dying*!" she moaned. Another boy slapped the counter angrily and declared that someone had stolen the hubcaps off his car.

Still Kate waited, clutching the crumpled banner.

"Can I help you?" a woman finally asked.

"I need to talk to the principal," Kate said bravely.

"What's this about?" the secretary asked. She pushed a pencil into her hair, folded her hands on the counter, and tilted her head as she looked at Kate.

"I need to talk to Mrs. Larkin about a case of bullying," Kate said. She set the crumpled banner on the counter and started to spread it out.

The secretary didn't even look at the banner. "Did someone get injured?" she asked.

"No," Kate replied, but then changed her mind because J.T.'s feelings had surely been hurt. "I mean yes! My brother!"

"Where is he?"

Kate had no idea of J.T.'s schedule. "In class somewhere."

"Does he need medical attention?"

It was Kate's turn to frown. "No . . ."

The secretary considered these answers. Then she walked to her desk, where she pulled out a drawer and returned to hand Kate a piece of paper.

Kate glanced at it: "Bullying, Cyberbullying, Harassment, or Intimidation Reporting Form."

"Fill this out and bring it back to the office," she said.

Kate hadn't realized she would have to fill out a form. She'd thought she could talk to someone. She *wanted* to talk to someone.

The form was two pages long and full of little boxes to check.

Name of Alleged Offender:

Is he/she a student? Yes / No

Place an x next to the statement that best describes what happened:

❑ **Any bullying, cyberbullying, harassment, or intimidation that involves physical aggression**

❑ **Getting another person to hit or harm the student**

❑ **Teasing, name-calling, making critical remarks, or threatening, in person or by other means**

That last one certainly fit, Kate thought. So did the next one.

❑ **Demeaning and making the victim of jokes**

She set her purse on the counter beside the crumpled banner and rummaged in a side pocket of her backpack for a pen so she could fill in the information.

"Wait a minute," the secretary said, stopping her. "What's your name?"

"Kate Tyler."

"Kate, listen to me, hon," the secretary said. "Take the form with you. Fill it out. Then return it to the office."

"But you have to do something *now*!"

The secretary held up both hands. "Take your time. Fill out the form and bring it back. That is the protocol. We need the form."

Protocol. That word again: *the rules of appropriate behavior.* "But this boy—"

"Look," the secretary's voice was firm when she cut Kate off. "Give us the information we need, and we'll follow up on it."

"What about the banner?" Kate asked, gently lifting the pile of papers.

But the secretary had moved on down the counter to the next student, who couldn't get his locker open.

Kate was a mix of anger, frustration, and now, disappointment. Pressed together, her lips made a tight line. Quickly, she gathered up the banner and left. She would take the form home and fill it out. She would follow the rules, the *protocol*, and Curtis Jenkins would be punished. Maybe even suspended.

On her way out of the office, Kate angrily stuffed the banner into the wastebasket, then, three steps into the hall, changed her mind and returned to pull it out, even taking the time to sit for a minute, smoothing out the papers and folding them so they'd fit into her backpack.

When she finished, she realized she was twenty minutes late for class and, shoulders slumped, returned to the counter to wait for a late pass.

~8~
A WEDGE

Our knowledge of biology helps us to understand how life on earth is connected," Mr. Rutkowski was telling his new biology class. Kate was relieved her teacher didn't question the late pass. He handed her a textbook, then a syllabus, and nodded toward a vacant seat.

"This knowledge of how life is connected can be used in many ways," her teacher continued.

Kate sat and placed the heavy textbook on her desk. A growling tiger stared back at her from the cover. Tigers were beautiful, even when they were angry. But they had a reason to be angry, Kate sympathized. All tigers were endangered. Out of nine subspecies of tigers, only six remained, and it was all because people not only destroyed their habitats but hunted them for pelts, meat, and body parts. She sighed and glanced at the open book on the boy's desk beside hers to try to figure out where they were. The boy smiled and pointed to the page number.

"Thanks," Kate mouthed. She flipped to the right page and shifted uncomfortably. She hoped she'd done the right thing marching into the office and getting that form. It wasn't like her to be so bold. But she was angry—like that tiger on the book cover! Maybe that's what anger did to a person. It made them do things they otherwise might never do. She thought of J.T. curling his fists in front of Curtis. And how she had called out "Who did this?"

"Advances in biology help us fight diseases," Mr. Rutkowski went on. "Diseases like cystic fibrosis and cancer."

Cancer. Kate blinked hard and tried to close a curtain on the hallway incident and endangered tigers and now, hearing the word cancer. She needed to focus on her class.

"Your diet and the chemicals that you are exposed to can affect whether or not you get a particular form of cancer," her teacher continued.

But there it was again. The word for the insidious disease that had taken away her father. Mr. Rutkowski had mentioned it twice already. Kate swallowed hard. She would never hear the word *cancer* again and not feel a punch to her stomach. From J.T.'s problems, to vanishing tigers, to cancer, to her father's death. Was she never going to have a normal day again? A normal *moment*?

Apparently, Mr. Rutkowski liked to walk while he talked. "For example," he said, now from the back of the room, "smokers often get lung cancer, which is caused by tobacco. Now they say there is a link between CT scans in children and leukemia, which is a different kind of cancer where white blood cells displace normal blood."

Kate stared at a spot beneath the front blackboard and thought back to early summer, just after J.T. had come home. The truck that delivered chicken feed to their farm was pumping it into the two large metal tanks on either side of the chicken houses; and the auger, the long, metal pipelike arm that transferred the feed from the truck to the bin, had not aligned properly, allowing some of the feed to spill out onto the roof and into the air. J.T. stood watching with his hands on his hips and a deep scowl on his face.

"What's wrong?" Kate asked him.

"See all that dust flying around?" he asked.

Kate looked again. "Yeah. I see it." She thought he was going to say that all that dust was a waste of money, but wouldn't that be the chicken company's loss? After all, they provided and paid for all the feed.

J.T.'s expression didn't change. "Could be what made Dad sick."

His reply shocked Kate. "What are you talking about? Chicken feed gave Dad kidney disease? And then cancer?"

J.T. lifted his shoulders and then lowered them. He didn't look at Kate. "Maybe."

Was he kidding? Why would he say that? Sometimes Kate had a really hard time figuring out her brother. "Well, I never saw him eat any of it!"

J.T. didn't think her reply was funny. "It's nothing he ever ate," he said. "It's what he breathed in all those years. Before this big truck here, before we were even born, they used to drop off bags of feed that Dad cut open with his jackknife and dumped into feed carts. The carts ran on a steel track into the chicken house, where he'd scoop it out into the feeders for the chickens. There was a lot of dust. Dad said some farmers he knew even wore masks. But he said no one ever thought back then that it was going to make them sick. They never even questioned the stuff the company put in the feed."

"What was in the feed that was so bad?"

"Chemicals."

"Chemicals," Kate repeated, holding her hands palm up. "What kind of chemicals?"

"You ever heard of arsenic?" J.T. asked her.

"Arsenic?" Kate's eyebrows shot up. "Sure! Arsenic is poison! But why would a chicken company put arsenic in the feed?"

J.T. smiled a little. A funny smile, though, like she couldn't possibly understand. "It's complicated," he said.

Kate was put out by his attitude. It made her feel dumb or like a little kid. Plus she still found the whole conversation weird. It was something else her brother probably wouldn't talk about again. Another subject off limits and unspoken, another brick in the wall he was building between them.

But now Mr. Rutkowski had mentioned the word *cancer*, and Kate couldn't help but think of her father's diagnosis of kidney disease, then kidney cancer and his last days struggling to breathe. Could there actually be something to J.T.'s puzzling comment? *See all that dust flying around?*

She would never forget. *Never.* For nearly two years, Kate's father had gone to the clinic three times a week for kidney dialysis. During the summer, Kate often went with him to keep him company and help him in and out of the county van. Sometimes, when he was on the machine that cleaned his blood, she read to him from the newspaper because he liked to keep up with the news. If he'd already seen the paper, then she'd get an old *National Geographic* from the basket at the clinic to read to him. She always went for the animal stories first: saving koala bears from the modern-day threats of highways and dogs, a beauty pageant for camels in Abu Dhabi, the zebras' epic migration as they followed the rains.

The dialysis took nearly four hours, so they also spent a chunk of time just sitting together. Kate always brought her journal. Writing in her journal that summer was when Kate discovered how suffering taught her to see the details . . .

I know it hurts, but Dad leans his head back and repeats Kerry's corny joke to Lisa, the nurse. "Why do we keep the refrigerator door closed?" he asks as Lisa sticks a needle into the gigantic, ropy vein called a fistula on my dad's arm. "I give up," Lisa says. Dad tells her, "Because the salad is dressing!" Lisa smiles and then slips another needle into Dad's arm. The needles are attached to long tubes that carry Dad's blood to the machine and then return it without the bad stuff that has been building up because Dad's kidneys don't work right.

My dad never complains. He never gets impatient the way I do. In my head, I can be somewhere else when I'm writing. But after I put the pen away, I keep an eye on the clock and get up to walk the clinic hallways, avoiding the lines bordering the squares of tile just for something to do.

After the van brings us home, my dad stretches back in his La-Z-Boy, and I pull the afghan up over his knees. "Thanks, Katie Bug," he says, and tries to squeeze my hand. No one except for my dad ever calls me Katie Bug, and I feel like crying, but not in front of him. I wish he could have a banana, because he loves bananas. But he can't eat them anymore. They contain a lot of potassium, and that's bad for people with kidney problems. Still, I wonder how much harm one single banana would do. When my eyes mist up, I turn the TV on to CNN and rush to the kitchen to measure out a small glass of orange juice instead.

"We don't have all the answers," a doctor had once told Kate while he tried to explain the kidney cancer and why her father had only a couple months to live. "I'm so sorry. There's nothing more we can do."

So *unfair*, people said.

Bad luck, others concluded as the illness took its toll.

After her father passed away, some people from church said, *It was his time*. Others tried to comfort Kate's family by saying it was all part of *God's plan*. But Kate could not accept that explanation. Despite the kindness and all the meals and prayers, the cancer had driven a wedge into her beliefs.

"Kate! Over here!" Jess called out in the noisy cafeteria.

When Kate finally made it through the lunchtime crowd, she saw that Jess had saved her a seat next to Olivia and across from two other girls Kate knew from middle school. Samantha and Lindsey were on the junior varsity field hockey team, too. Both were on the forward line. Lindsey had an especially powerful drive. Everyone hoped she was going to score a lot of points this season. Sam and Lindsey hadn't been good friends with Jess and Kate back in eighth grade. They'd always been what Kate and Jess called "the popular girls." But it was the second day of high school, and maybe everyone was just trying to find a place to fit in. They had field hockey in common. Maybe they'd be the field hockey group. Kate kind of liked the idea.

"Hi!" she greeted them.

Kate pulled out the chair and sat down. But before she even put her lunch bag on the table, the girls peppered her with questions.

"So what was the deal with your brother this morning?" Sam asked.

"Yeah. What did the sign say?" Lindsey chimed in. "That J.T. is a jerk?"

"Or a dumb ass. I heard it called your brother a dumb ass," Sam added as she peeled the wrapper around an ice-cream sandwich.

Surprised, Kate stopped scooting the chair up to the table and held the lunch bag on her lap. "The sign didn't have any cusswords in it," she said.

"The sign said Chicken Man. 'The Chicken Man Returns,'" Olivia noted matter-of-factly.

Jess met Kate's eyes. "It's so awful," she said. "Is J.T. okay?"

But there was no time to respond to Jess, because Lindsey had leaned toward Kate from across the table and asked, "Is it true you yanked it off the wall and threw it at Curtis?"

"I heard you slapped him," Sam added with a chuckle.

"No!" Kate told them. "I didn't throw it! I didn't slap any-body!"

"He is such a jerk, though," Lindsey said. "He deserved it! J.T. should have punched him out."

Olivia rolled her eyes. "It's just drama, you guys. That's all it is. There was a lot of drama like that in my old middle school."

"No. It's more than drama," Kate disagreed. "Curtis isn't going to leave my brother alone until someone stops him. I feel like the school needs to step in."

Lindsey smiled like she was truly amused. "You know what my dad would say? It's life, and you got to get tough. If someone's picking on you, let 'em have it. That's what he told my brother. Last year—my brother, who's a junior this year—he beat up this kid who was bugging him."

Sam was nodding. "Yeah, my dad says all that anti-bully stuff is crap—"

"No!" Kate shook her head.

"It's not crap, Lindsey!" Jess interjected, backing up Kate.

Lindsey just shrugged. "Whatever." She pulled open a bag of chips and started eating them.

"So do you think there's going to be a fight?" Sam asked around a mouthful of ice-cream sandwich. "Like after school or something?"

"Probably," Lindsey said as she offered her chips to the group.

"A fight?" Kate's mouth fell open. She turned from Sam and Lindsey to Jess with a painful look.

"Guys, maybe Kate doesn't want to talk about this right now," Jess said.

"It's just drama," Olivia repeated as she dipped into the chip bag Lindsey offered.

But now Kate was worried that something terrible would happen to J.T. after school. He was planning to stay for a science club meeting. If he did, then he would be waiting on the bench outside school for their grandmother to pick them up. He would be a sitting duck for someone like Curtis. If he got into any kind of trouble, he'd be sent back to juvenile detention.

For a moment no one said anything. Lindsey munched her chips. Olivia sipped her strawberry milk. Sam redid her long ponytail. And Jess watched Kate. None of them really cared about what happened to J.T., did they? Maybe Jess did, Kate thought, but not the others. They just wanted the gossip, the inside scoop to fuel "the drama." That's all it was.

The paper bag with Kate's peanut butter sandwich suddenly felt heavy in her hand. Slowly, she nestled it down inside the backpack.

"I just realized I left my lunch in my locker," Kate said.

Jess looked alarmed. "But—"

"It's okay. I'll be right back," Kate said.

But she wouldn't return. She was on a mission now. She picked up her things and left.

~9~
A MATTER OF TIME

Kate rushed straight to the girls' room, where she entered a stall and closed the door. Two girls standing near a sink looked startled when she burst in. The smell of cigarette smoke lingered in the air. After latching the door, Kate pulled out the bullying report form and a book to write on, tucked in her skirt and sat on the toilet. She coughed a little so the girls might think she was sick, then focused on the questions and began filling in the answers with a pen.

What did the alleged offender do or say?

Easy enough. Kate described the banner strung across the hallway.

Did a physical injury result from this incident?

If there was a physical injury, do you think there will be permanent effects?

Was the student victim absent from school as a result of the incident?

No. No. And no.

If none of these things had happened, maybe the report wouldn't be taken seriously. Kate frowned and pressed a hand to her forehead. But wasn't the whole point of the form to stop those things from happening?

Did a psychological injury result from this incident?

Maybe. It was possible! But how would Kate know? She tapped the pen on the palm of her hand as she read the next question.

Is there any additional information you would like to provide?

Yes, there was. Kate wrote about how Curtis had bullied J.T. in middle school and how her brother had just returned from nearly a year in juvenile detention. He served time for what he did, Kate wrote. He wants to start over, but how can he with Curtis picking on him all the time?

When she finished, Kate started to read everything over again, but the buzzer sounded and lunch was over. She clicked her pen and put it away.

Walking fast, she went directly to the office to hand in the form. The secretary she had spoken with earlier took the paperwork. "That was fast," she said. "I'll be sure this goes to the right person."

Kate heaved a sigh of relief.

It was just a matter of time, then.

Throughout her first geometry class (mostly review), then Chinese (*ni hao*—"hello") then field hockey practice, Kate tried to focus, but she was distracted with worry.

"Why didn't you come back to lunch?" Jess asked, looking

anxious as the two girls changed up for practice.

"I guess I lost my appetite," Kate said.

Jess leaned in and whispered, "Sorry about Sam and Lindsey. That was mean."

Kate shrugged. "Don't worry about it," she said, closing up her locker. She walked away to stand in front of a mirror where she made two short pigtails to keep the hair out of her face. There were larger concerns on Kate's mind. She didn't want J.T. to be involved in a fight after school.

Throughout practice, Kate kept glancing at her watch. When the drills ran longer than J.T.'s meeting, she ran to the sideline.

"You have to leave? What for?" Coach Dietrich asked.

Kate knew this wouldn't be easy. Her coach was really nice. Just last week she'd had the entire team over to her town house to cook hot dogs on her grill. She had made all kinds of salads and even bought ice cream for the girls. But she was totally serious on the field and incredibly strict about practice.

"You didn't bring me a note," Coach Dietrich said before Kate had a chance to say anything more.

Nervous, Kate pulled on one of her pigtails. Should she say she had a dentist appointment? No. Kate didn't want to lie. "It's a family thing," she said, forcing herself to maintain eye contact.

The coach studied Kate. "All right," she said. "Just this once, Kate. Go ahead."

"Thank you. Thank you so much!"

Kate whirled around and started running back to the gym when the coach called out, "Tomorrow let's try you out in a halfback position, okay?"

Turning, Kate smiled broadly. "Oh, my gosh, yes! Thank you so much!"

Back in the locker room, Kate skipped the shower and just grabbed her stuff and a bottle of cold water from the cooler by the coach's door. Rushing out to the front of the school, she saw J.T. sitting alone on a bench near the flagpole. Their grandmother was picking them up that day, since Jess had to go straight from practice to an orthodontist appointment.

"Hey, how was science club?" she asked, still breathless, but relieved she'd arrived before anything bad could happen.

J.T. was bent over his homework. "Okay."

Kate dropped her stuff on the ground and collapsed beside her brother on the bench. "Are there some nice kids?" She took a swig of water.

"Don't know, Kate. Not really there for friends. I've got a project I really want to get done."

"Oh." Kate took another long drink and then held the cold plastic bottle against her face. She wondered what project he was talking about, but he had his graphing calculator out and seemed pretty engrossed in his homework, so she didn't ask. Instead, she took out her American history textbook and a yellow highlighter.

The blare of a horn interrupted them. Kate and J.T. looked up to see Curtis Jenkins slow down in front of them in a green pickup truck. Hooper Delaney sat beside him. If he was old enough to drive, then Curtis was at least sixteen and a half, Kate thought. He must've had to stay back a year, which didn't surprise her at all.

"Yo!" he called out while his truck rolled to a stop. He actually stuck his hand out the window and held it up as though in greeting.

Kate stood up defiantly. Was he going to pick a fight?

Just then, the front doors of the school opened. A kid and what appeared to be a parent walked out. The doors closed heavily behind them.

"Let's go inside," Kate urged J.T. "We can watch for Grandma from the window."

But J.T. didn't move. Calmly, he turned his attention to homework again.

As the other people came down the sidewalk, Curtis pulled his arm back in. "Later!" he called before slowly moving on.

Relief. But only for the moment, because what did "later" mean?

J.T. was doing a great job of ignoring the situation, Kate thought, a little annoyed. Maybe he had escaped this time, but Kate knew Curtis wouldn't quit. She was glad—*very glad*—she had turned in that form.

Suddenly, Kate noticed that J.T. was not only staring at something behind her, he was slowly standing up, the calculator still in his hand.

The kid who had come out of school was Brady. Brady Parks and his mom stood a few feet away.

Kate stopped breathing. The boys hadn't seen each other since that day in court over a year ago. She watched Brady's eyes flick from Curtis's departing pickup truck to J.T. Had he heard Curtis call out? Did Brady catch who it was?

Time seemed to stand still. It was Mrs. Parks who spoke first. "J.T., it's good to see you," she said with a gentle smile. "Welcome home."

God bless Brady's Mom, Kate thought. She let out her breath.

Brady was wearing the Corsica High soccer uniform, green shorts and a gold and green top. He must have made the team and just come in from practice. His face was sweaty—his hair, too, and some of it was stuck to the side of his face. He took an uncertain step forward. "Yeah, welcome back," he said to J.T. "And hey, thanks for that letter."

"You're welcome," J.T. replied. "Thanks for writing back. It meant a lot."

The two boys looked at each other. Kate wondered what they had written to each other and what they were thinking. There didn't seem to be any anger. Were they glad to see each other? Or were they just being polite?

The tense moment became almost unbearable when Brady glanced at Kate. Already flushed, she felt even more blood rush to her face. When Brady actually smiled a little and the corners of his mouth turned upward, she was so overcome with emotion she had to look away.

"Well, see you around, both you guys," Brady said.

J.T. nodded. "Yeah, see you around."

Both you guys. Brady's words echoed in Kate's head.

And that was it. Brady and his mom left.

"Let me see: soup, bread, salad, iced tea. That's it." Kate's grandmother surveyed the tray she had placed in Kate's hands that evening. Somehow, it had become Kate's job to deliver dinner to her mother whenever she had a headache.

Kate accepted the tray with a glum expression, but only because she was still distracted by events at school.

Her grandmother misread Kate's thoughts. "I know, I know. We're enabling her, aren't we?" she said. "We should stop and force your mother to come downstairs if she wants to eat."

Kate wasn't sure what *enabling* meant, but she had a pretty good idea it had something to do with making it easy for her mother to avoid facing her problems.

"I tell you what. We're going to stop this right now." She took the tray out of Kate's hands and placed it on the counter. "Run up and tell your mother dinner's ready. If she's hungry, she can come down and eat."

Kate did as she was told, and everyone except for her mother ate. Afterward, Kate helped with the dishes and then launched into homework. She finished assignments for English and American history, then texted Jess about some math problems. She gathered her outfit for the game, putting a clean uniform in her field hockey bag and plucking some green and gold hair ribbons from a basket on her bureau. Finally, she sat cross-legged on her bed, her school journal open to an empty page on the pillow in front of her. The assignment for creative writing was to "describe a special place."

Whenever I need to get away, I follow the dirt path between corn and soybean fields all the way down to the river to sit on the fallen locust tree. The trunk that juts over the water is my special place. Straddling it, I love to dangle my bare feet and daydream. . . .

Kate paused and thought back to once when J.T. came with her and they shared their dreams. It must have been more than a year ago, because it was before J.T. got into trouble.

"For sure I want to go to college," Kate had told him. "Then I want to be a linguist."

"A linguist, what's that? Someone who makes linguine?" J.T. had asked.

"Ha, ha. Very funny," Kate replied. Her smile faltered. "Are you kidding? You don't know what a linguist is?" It wasn't often Kate knew something that J.T. didn't.

Her brother grinned. "Someone who studies language."

"Okay, but did you know that elephants have a language?"

J.T. dropped his chin and looked at her over his glasses.

"Seriously," Kate said. "Elephants make these rumbling sounds that are so low humans can't even hear them. They talk to one another!"

"And what are they saying, Kate?"

"Maybe they're saying, 'Watch out for that man with a rifle. I think he wants to kill me so somebody can carve an ivory statue out of my tusk.'"

"Sad," J.T. acknowledged.

"It is! I really want to help them. I'm not afraid to go live in the jungle! For a while anyway. If I had to. If there was, like, a house or something. But do you think I'd need to be a linguist or a scientist to study elephant language?"

"I don't know," he told her, "but for sure you'd have to be crazy."

Kate had laughed. But she knew J.T. took all of her "animal passions" (his term) seriously. He had helped her make an impressive graph for her fifth-grade report that demonstrated the speed with which the ice caps were melting and the polar bears vanishing. And he was the one who came up with the idea of a trip to the National Zoo to see the baby panda when Kate turned eight.

"So what do *you* want to do?" Kate had asked her brother.

After handing Kate his glasses so he could hang upside down from their tree, J.T. confided to her how he wanted to be a professional hacker, one of those cyber experts at the National Security Agency who helped protect the country.

"You got to keep that a secret, though," he told her, pulling himself back upright on the branch, his face flushed red with the blood that had run to his head. "Promise me? Because you know Dad wants me to take over the farm. I hate to let him down, but, man, I do not want to raise chickens."

No! Kate shook her head vehemently. Neither did she! She had handed him his glasses back . . .

What would become of their dreams now? Kate wondered, still holding the pen over the single paragraph she'd written in her school journal. Would their precious hopes be swallowed up by all the larger worries?

Frustrated because she didn't have the answer, Kate paused to look out the window at the foot of her bed. While it was dark out, there was moonlight, too, and she thought she saw someone running across the yard. On her stomach, she scooted closer to the window. Was it her brother? It looked like him. Why would J.T. be running at night? Where had he been?

Down the hall, Kate's mother was silent behind her closed door and Kate's grandmother was reading a story to Kerry.

Kate stepped into her flip-flops and rushed downstairs.

Outside, the early September evening was still warm. Crickets chirped in the soybean fields, and the chicken smell was faint. She spotted her brother, a dark profile, sitting on the gas tank down by the tractor sheds. When she got closer, she could see Tucker curled up on the ground and noticed that J.T. was facing in the direction of Brady's house next door. It used to be you could see a dirt path made by the two boys going back and forth through the field, but not anymore.

Had J.T. run over there? To Brady's house? Was he running to get in shape? *To fight Curtis?* All kinds of crazy thoughts ran through her mind. She stooped to pick up a tiny stone and threw it, making it ping off the tank.

J.T. didn't move.

"Whatcha doin'?" Kate asked.

"Nothin' much," J.T. said.

He was still breathing hard. Kate could smell his sweat.

"Where have you been?" she asked.

"For a run."

She wanted to ask why but didn't want to seem pushy. She climbed up onto the gas tank and sat beside him.

After a long moment, J.T. said, "Sometimes I wish I wasn't here anymore."

"Don't say that!" Kate exclaimed, nudging him with her elbow. "Things will get better!" She was desperate to say something encouraging, but at a loss as to what it might be. "Just focus on doing well in school, J.T."

Her brother ran a hand across his mouth, but he didn't say anything.

"Remember that day we were watching TV and they interviewed that homeless girl?" she asked him. "She lived in a car with her parents and brushed her teeth at the gas station? Remember how she won a science competition at her school and got a college scholarship? She said that despite how bad everything gets, you have to stay focused. You can't give up hope."

J.T. finally turned to face her. "Yeah, well I'm trying to do good, Kate, but I can't get traction. How can I make a new start with Curtis dragging me down?"

"Did something else happen?"

He shook his head slightly. "Just little stuff."

"That's why you need to tell someone, J.T. *Tell* them what Curtis is doing, so they'll make him stop!"

"But they can't stop him, Kate! If I complain, everything gets worse. Plus I don't want to be seen by everybody as *the victim*. It's bad enough the way people see me. I don't want to be pitied and hated both."

"No one hates you, J.T.," Kate declared.

"Of course they do!"

"Well, you're *wrong*!" Kate insisted, although she didn't mean to raise her voice.

"Yeah! Probably I'm wrong, Kate," J.T. snapped sarcastically. "It wouldn't be the first time, would it?" He slid off the tank.

Kate didn't respond. She knew he was referring to his decision to help sabotage the red kayak which caused the death of a little boy and landed J.T. in juvenile detention. Biggest mistake he'd ever made in his life. No question about it. The tragic loss of Benjamin DiAngelo and her brother's conviction for second-degree murder was always going to be a cloud over his life—

over *all* their lives, including her own. Kate knew people looked at her differently. Not long after J.T. left, she was at the 7-Eleven picking out a Snapple, when she heard a boy in the pretzel aisle behind her, whisper to a friend, *"That girl? Her brother was one of the kids who killed the little boy."* When she closed the cooler door, the kids took off.

When J.T. started walking back toward the house with Tucker at his heels, Kate didn't try to stop him. Watching him go, she wondered if she was always going to be *that girl*, the brother of *that boy*.

Sometimes Kate got angry because it was so unfair. But she could never figure out who to blame. Whose fault was it? Would *time* make it go away? The passage of time? If so, then how long would it take for people to forget?

Or *forgive*?

Even after the screen door slammed shut up at the house, Kate stood in the dark, listening to the crickets. How was this all going to end? As bad as it was for her, it had to be ten times worse for J.T.

Maybe it was her imagination, but it seemed like the insects' noise grew louder, and louder still, until it was almost deafening and Kate had to cover her ears.

~10~
IMPOSSIBLE

Kate, listen to me!" Jess demanded. She turned on the bus seat to face Kate.

"I'm sorry. What?" Kate asked.

"Just *tell* me. Do you want to go to the pep rally after school?"

"The pep rally," Kate repeated.

"The pep rally for the first football game! Kate! Come on. Just answer me yes or no. Olivia keeps asking me, but I don't want to go if you're not going."

Kate finally focused on her friend's pained expression. Did Jess have mascara on her eyelashes?

"You're like a space cadet, Kate! I mean, why *wouldn't* you want to go? It's our first pep rally! There's no field hockey practice. It'll be fun!"

Kate turned away. Jess was changing. Was it Olivia?

"Kate?"

"I don't know yet," Kate said.

Jess sighed and fell back against the seat. "Well, let me know by noon, okay? I need to call my mom and ask her if she can come get us."

"Okay."

Jess turned to look out the window then, and the girls didn't talk anymore all the way to school. Kate didn't mean to ignore Jess or put her off. She certainly didn't want to hurt her feelings—or worse yet, lose her as a friend, but it was impossible to focus on a pep rally when she was wondering if today was the day she'd be called down to the office for her bullying report. Would they talk to her alone? With J.T.? With *both* boys? Would someone call her mother? If they needed her mother to go to the school, would she be able to leave the house?

Even in biology lab, where Mr. Rutkowski was reading off names and assigning lab partners for the semester, Kate was only half tuned in.

"What's your last name again?"

Kate looked up at the boy standing beside her at the lab table. The boy with dark curly hair who had shown her the page number on the first day of school. He seemed really nice, and now she was noticing that he had soft brown eyes and cute dimples in his cheeks.

"Did you say Taylor?" he asked.

"No, Tyler," Kate replied. She spelled it for him. "And your name again? I'm sorry, I didn't catch everything."

"Oh, yeah, sure. It's Marc—with a *c*," he said, pointing at her notes when she wrote it as Mark. "Last name is Connors."

"Were you at Corsica Middle last year?" Kate asked.

He shook his head. "I'm new this year. I moved here from Oregon."

"Oregon," Kate repeated. "Wow. That's pretty far away."

Suddenly, the intercom blinked and the office secretary's voice came on.

Kate froze, knowing the call would be for her. In slow motion, she closed her notebook and clicked her pen shut.

The secretary's voice was shrill: "I'm sorry for the interruption, Mr. Rutkowski, but could you please send Marc Connors to the office for dismissal?"

Surprised, Kate looked at Marc.

He arched his eyebrows and grinned. "That would be me. Gotta go." He leaned toward Kate. "Take good notes, okay? Maybe we can get together and go over stuff later this week."

Kate nodded numbly. "Sure." She watched Marc from Oregon slide his book off the desk and leave the room.

The day dragged on after that. Kate never was called to the office. The only exciting thing happened in the afternoon, when Curtis Jenkins showed up in Kate's Creative Writing class.

Stunned, she watched in disbelief as Mr. Ellison gave Curtis a syllabus and spoke quietly to him before indicating an empty desk up front. Curtis may have seen her on his way to sit down, but how would she know? She had covered her mouth and turned completely away.

Mr. Ellison wrote a phrase on the board: *My reason for being here.* Then he ordered the students to take out their journals and start writing.

Heads bent and pens and pencils moved across paper. Kate

had to pull herself together and write, too. She reconsidered the phrase, *my reason for being here*, and wondered if Mr. Ellison meant the reason for being in his class, or if he was after a more cosmic meaning, such as the reason for life itself. Kate had always wanted to be a writer ever since she was about five years old, when she was folding paper to make little books. She'd start with that.

"Mr. Jenkins, you're not writing," Mr. Ellison observed.

Kate glanced over.

"No, sir," Curtis answered. He was stretched back in his chair, his long legs protruding into the aisle, but he straightened up some as he spoke. "Only reason I'm here is 'cause they didn't have no place else for me to go. Period. End of story."

A few kids chuckled.

Kate rolled her eyes.

"Well, there you go, Mr. Jenkins," the writing teacher replied. "Where there is an end, there is almost always a whole new beginning." He handed Curtis a piece of paper. "Write about your new beginning and what you're thinking."

By the afternoon, Kate had totally forgotten about the pep rally. Upset about finding Curtis in her class and frustrated that there had been no action on her report, she practically ran to the bus after school. Only then did she realize she had never even given an answer to Jess. She covered her face with one hand and sank back against the seat.

J.T. had skipped the pep rally, too. But Kate didn't see the bruise on his face until they both got home.

"What's that?" she asked, horrified by the puffy black and blue skin halfway closing his left eye.

"I fell in gym," he mumbled, turning away.

Kate didn't believe him. Not for a second. It didn't look like the kind of injury you'd get playing soccer.

The next day, a Saturday, Kate learned the truth about the bruise. In the backseat of her grandmother's car, she was plugged into her phone listening to music when a text came.

Jess: Hey. What are you doing?

It didn't sound like Jess was mad. Amazing. She was an amazing friend.

Kate: Errands with my grandma.

Jess: Missed you last night at the football game. ☹

Kate: Sorry I never got back to you.

Jess: No worries.

Kate: Was the game fun?

Jess: Crazy. Some kids got in trouble for drinking.

Kate: Yikes.

Jess: Hope J.T.'s okay. I heard he got stuffed into a gym locker yesterday.

Kate's hands went limp.

In Chestertown, Kate's grandmother parked the car on the street in front of the Dunkin' Donuts. J.T.'s probation officer had her office above the doughnut shop.

"I want a honey dip!" Kerry called out.

While Kerry and her grandmother went to get drinks and

doughnuts to pass the time, Kate went upstairs with J.T. She had waited for her brother once before at Miss Hatcher's office, and she knew that when the waiting room was quiet you could hear through the walls.

Kate was glad to see that no one else was there. As soon as J.T. went into Miss Hatcher's office and closed the door behind him, Kate pulled her earphones out and wrapped them around her phone.

"So what happened to your eye?" Miss Hatcher asked.

Kate leaned forward from her seat on the couch to listen.

"I fell playing soccer in gym," J.T. replied, but so softly that Kate could barely hear him.

Miss Hatcher didn't argue, and there was a pause. She didn't believe him either, Kate thought.

"J.T., tell me. How are things going at school?"

Kate stood and tiptoed to the door so she could hear better. She hoped this wasn't wrong. She was only eavesdropping to make sure that J.T. leveled with Miss Hatcher—so he could get the help he needed. If Miss Hatcher knew the truth, maybe she could step in and talk with the principal. Maybe she could even get him transferred to another school.

"Things at school are great," J.T. said.

Astonished, Kate let her mouth fall open.

"I'm really involved in this science project," he continued with what Kate thought was faked enthusiasm. "What I'm planning to do is test samples of chicken manure to see what the birds are eating."

He was changing the subject!

"And why would that be important, J.T.?" she asked.

Miss Hatcher was falling for it! Angry, Kate lifted her fist to knock on the door.

"You may not know this, but in the past, some growers have actually put arsenic in their chicken feed," J.T. said.

Kate stopped herself from knocking in order to listen.

"They're not supposed to put that stuff in the feed anymore, but I thought I'd do this study on it to check and see, because if there's still arsenic getting fed to chickens, it can affect people who eat their meat."

"Is that so?" Miss Hatcher asked. "Arsenic in chicken feed? Why would anyone do that, J.T.?"

Kate brought her hand down. That was what she was wondering, too.

"Here's the thing," J.T. said, sounding very sure of himself. "The arsenic doesn't kill the chickens, but it kills this bug in the chicken's gut. So the chickens grow faster. The arsenic is still in their bodies, though. And if it is, it could be in the meat you buy at the store or eat in a restaurant. And that kind of arsenic can cause cancer in people."

"You don't say."

"The other thing," J.T. continued, "is that the arsenic makes blood vessels burst in the chicken, which makes their meat look pink and plump. People see it at the grocery store, and they think, wow, this meat is nice and healthy. They don't know it's burst blood vessels."

"What in the world got you started on this?" Miss Hatcher asked, and there was a leathery squeak, like she either leaned back or sat up in her chair.

A long pause. "My father," J.T. finally told her.

It became quiet on the other side of the wall.

"You must miss your dad," Miss Hatcher sympathized.

"I do," J.T. said. "I wish my dad was here." When his voice grew high and tight, like he was trying hard not to cry, Kate's eyes blurred with tears, too.

"I never got a chance to say good-bye to him," J.T. said.

Another squeak and footsteps told Kate Miss Hatcher had gotten up. Maybe she was handing her brother a tissue. Or putting her arm around his shoulders.

Quickly, Kate wiped at her eyes with the edge of one hand and tiptoed back to the couch where she sat, unwrapping and plugging her earphones back in so they wouldn't think she'd overheard.

At home that night, after everyone else had gone to bed, J.T. took off on his bicycle in the dark. From her bedroom window, Kate watched him leave, then, worried, went outside to sit on the porch, where she waited nearly an hour for his return. She watched as he walked his bike into one of the tractor sheds and noticed that as he got close to the house, he pushed a small bag into his pocket.

"Where did you go?" she asked, walking the short distance to meet him and trying to sound casual.

Still breathing a bit heavily, J.T. settled his hands on his hips. "Just for a ride," he said. "To clear my head."

Uncertain of what to think or do, Kate turned and walked back up the porch steps with J.T. Was there something new to worry about? What if that little bag he'd shoved in his pocket was drugs? She'd seen a boy with a bag of something green on the school bus once. Even if it had turned out to be just oregano—a big joke—some people had thought it was real marijuana. It was in a little plastic bag like the one she'd seen in J.T.'s hand.

"I know how you got the bruise," she declared, desperate to say or do something that would stop her brother from getting into trouble.

J.T. paused at the front door and turned around.

"I'm going to the office," she blurted. "I'm going to report Curtis!"

He shook his head. "No you're not."

"Well, maybe I already have!"

J.T.'s voice stayed calm. "I know you have. I got called down to the guidance office because of that form you filled out."

"So what happened?" she demanded.

"*Nothing* happened."

"What do you mean, *nothing happened*? Is Curtis in trouble?"

"No."

"Why not?"

"Because I denied it!" J.T. proclaimed.

Kate was flabbergasted. "You *denied* it? You told them none of that happened?"

"Yeah. I did."

"Then I'll take them that banner and show them myself!"

"What banner?" he challenged.

"The banner Curtis strung up!"

"I don't know what you're talking about!"

Kate ran ahead of him into the house and dashed upstairs to her room where she had left her backpack on the floor by her desk. Kneeling, she zipped it open and riffled through it. But the folded banner was gone. When she turned, she saw that J.T. had followed her into the room and closed the door.

"You took it!" she accused, jumping to her feet.

J.T. put his hands on her shoulders. "You need to butt out, Kate. Let me handle this!"

"But I can't—"

"That's it, Kate!" J.T. cut her off. "Stay out of it!"

When he walked back out, he closed the door so hard, Kate's grandmother called out from her bedroom, "Hey! Who's slamming doors?"

Stay out of it. The words echoed in her head. But how could Kate stay out of it when J.T.'s world was disintegrating before her eyes?

At lunch on Monday, Kate and Jess watched as Curtis and Hooper stole all the extra chairs at the small table where J.T. sat so no one else could sit with him even if they had wanted. At field hockey practice, Kate struggled not to cry when she heard that in J.T.'s study hall, kids were clucking like chickens.

That night when Kate went looking for J.T., she found him sitting outside his bedroom window on the roof. Kate crawled out and sat down beside him. The shingles were still warm from the hot day, and above them, the endless night sky was speckled by a million pinpricks of light.

"Hey," she said softly.

But J.T. had shut down and didn't answer. Her brother was probably the tallest kid in his class, but that night he seemed small sitting hunched over with his knees drawn up and his face hidden in his folded arms.

Kate put a hand on his shoulder and leaned in close. "It'll be okay," she whispered. But she didn't know if it would be.

The next day, J.T. was too sick to go to school.

"Do you know what's wrong?" Kate's grandmother asked after J.T. drank some orange juice and went back to bed holding his throat.

Yes, Kate imagined saying. *I do know what's wrong.* Her grandmother would pull out a chair and sit down to listen. But really, Kate thought, what could her grandmother *do*? And did Kate really want her involved? J.T. would be furious.

Still, it was tempting. Kate finished pouring milk on her cereal and gazed at the back of her grandmother, who stood at the sink, encased in her fuzzy, pink bathrobe, washing off the tips of her fingers. She was wearing the brace she sometimes put on her left wrist, which meant her carpal tunnel must be hurting again. And she'd slept funny, because her short gray hair was parted and flat, like a cowlick, in one spot on the back of her head. Sometimes, Grandma had a hard time sleeping—"fitful," she called it—and got up in the middle of the night to eat a piece of toast and work on a crossword puzzle. No way was Kate going to ask any more of her. She was already doing so much for them, plus she had Kate's grandfather to worry about. Every night she called him. *Did you take your heart medicine? Did you remember that the garbage goes out on Wednesday? Don't forget to bring the bins in.*

"Other than that sore throat, your brother seems fine,"

Grandma said, turning from the sink while she dried her fingertips on a small towel. "No fever. No chills." With a furrowed brow, she looked at Kate. "Are things okay at school?"

Quickly, Kate shoved in a spoonful of cereal and kind of shrugged, a cop-out, she was well aware, as she pointed to her full mouth.

"I'm concerned about that boy," Grandma said as she walked to the stove to cook an egg.

Kate swallowed and pushed the cereal around in her bowl. She wondered what it was going to take to stop Curtis. Because if the people at school wouldn't stop him, then who would? And *how*?

It seemed an impossible situation, Kate thought. Until Curtis himself offered the solution.

~11~
A PROPOSITION

Kate, slow down! I want to talk to you."

It was Curtis Jenkins. His voice saying her name sent a chill through Kate and almost made her stumble. She hadn't realized he even *knew* her name.

"Kate!" he called again as they left the Creative Writing classroom and merged into the stream of hallway traffic. When he tapped her on the shoulder—*he actually touched her*—every muscle in her body tensed. Kate pressed the books she was carrying tight against her chest and plunged into the mass of kids squeezing through a double doorway.

But she couldn't escape. Curtis quickly caught up. "I need to talk to you," he said over her shoulder. His hot breath on her neck made her cringe.

"Come on, Kate. I have a deal for you," he murmured.

Kate kept moving.

"Actually more like a proposition," he added, staying right behind her.

A *deal*? A *proposition*? What in the heck did that mean? Panicked, Kate pushed so hard through the crowd she knocked a girl's purse off her shoulder.

"Hey!" the girl said.

"Sorry," Kate said. She tried a different angle through the knot of students, but Curtis was like a leech she couldn't shake. Finally, she swung around and told him, "Leave me alone!"

"Shhhh! Calm down!" Curtis urged her, one hand pumping toward the floor.

"And lay off J.T.!" Kate fired back. "He didn't do anything to you!"

"Give me a second, will you?" Curtis drew his head back and grinned. "You know, you're kind of cute, Kate, when you get all mad like this."

Kate felt the warm rush of blood to her face. His out-of-line compliment only infuriated her more. She had half a mind to slap him across the face—or stomp on his foot! Instead, she took a deep breath and forced a calm voice. "Curtis Jenkins, stop torturing my brother."

"But that's what I'm trying to tell you!" Curtis exclaimed. When he leaned toward her again, his eyebrows went up beneath the wispy blond hair that fell over his face. "I *will* stop." The corners of his mouth lifted slightly. "I will—that is, if you do something for me."

Kate took another step back, but bumped into the wall.

Curtis moved forward so he was right in her face again. He was so close that Kate could see his intense blue eyes and a narrow scar over his left eyebrow. "If you write that assignment for me, I'll leave your wimpy brother alone."

Speechless, Kate stared at him.

A silly, lopsided smile spread over Curtis's face.

Incredible. He wanted her to write a paper for *him*?

"You are truly despicable, Curtis," she said, narrowing her eyes.

"Whoa!" Curtis reeled away and broke up laughing. A fake laugh, though, Kate could tell.

"*Truly despicable?* Wow! That's pretty strong, Kate!" He pointed at her. "You know I could report you to the principal for using language like that."

"I wouldn't do anything for you. Not if my life depended on it!" She practically spit the words out as she brushed past him.

"Yeah, well think about it!" he called after her.

No. She was not going to think about it, she said to herself as she rushed down the nearby stairs. But her mind was spinning anyway. The assignment was simple: *Pretend you're an author and write your own author's note, the stuff on the book flap. Tell us about yourself in third person and write it in a way that connects you to the topic of your new book. No more than 250 words.* She could write that piece for Curtis's book called *How to Be a Bully*. The essay would practically write itself. Two pages that would end her brother's torment.

Kate had to shake her head to get rid of the thought trying to worm its way into her brain. Because no way. It would be cheating, and Kate was *not* a cheater.

"Lots of garlic. Don't be shy. I always put three or four cloves of it in," Kate's grandmother instructed her. That evening, she and Kate were making J.T.'s favorite spaghetti meal again, this time with ice cream and chocolate sauce for dessert. While no one said so, Kate knew it was because J.T. would have to stay up most of the night supervising what the farmers called "chickens going out" or what the chicken company called "movement." When the chickens were seven weeks old, they were rounded up and taken to the processing plant. Several men came out to do the work, usually in the middle of the night when the chickens were apt to be quieter.

"Will you try to get some sleep before they come?" Grandma asked J.T. as they finished their meal. It had been a hot and humid day, and a fan was humming on the kitchen counter behind them, cooling them off slightly.

"Maybe," J.T. replied, resting his spoon with a clink in the empty ice-cream dish. "Sometimes it's easier to just stay up."

"Have the feeders been raised?" their mother asked. She was coming to dinner almost all the time now.

"Feeders have been up since this morning," J.T. told her.

Withholding feed from the birds assured that they wouldn't have anything in their stomachs the day they were taken for slaughter.

Angela pushed her chair back. "Well. Good luck with it," she said. "I hope you'll excuse me. I've got a terrible headache."

After taking her plate to the kitchen counter, their mother went upstairs. The night the chickens went out had always been difficult for her even in better times. It wasn't that she had refused to help over the years; their father had actually forbidden her from ever going near the chicken houses. Even after he got sick, their mother was never asked to help out. Responsibility for that went to J.T., and after he was sent away, Uncle Ray stepped in. "It's not your mother's job," Kate's dad always said. But Kate knew it went deeper than that.

"I'm going out to recheck everything," J.T. said, putting on his baseball cap. When he opened the door, they could hear raindrops hitting the back porch. Kate hoped the rain would cool things off.

After putting leftovers away, Kate sat back down at the table in front of the fan to finish writing the recipe for the spaghetti sauce.

"Two kinds of meat, remember. Ground beef *and* hot sausage," Kate's grandmother said as she dried the pasta pot. "A green pepper is good, too."

Add a green pepper, Kate wrote, leaning her head on one hand and slowly writing with the other.

"Kate, dear, what's wrong?" her grandmother asked.

She wrinkled her nose and sat up. "Nothing, really. I just don't want to have to do all the cooking again."

Grandma put down the pot and came to sit beside Kate. "No. I don't want you to have to do all the cooking either," she said quietly. "And I don't think you'll have to. But I've got to go home to North Carolina. Your grandfather needs me, too. If your mother has a relapse, you'll have to help out until I get back. Your mom's doing so much better, Kate. She's trying. But if she stops taking her medicine, she could get depressed and anxious again. It's a delicate balance, like walking a tightrope."

"I understand," Kate said, but she didn't really. Even when her mother took her medicine every day, it didn't seem to make her all better. She was taking on more of her old chores, it was true, but she still wouldn't drive the car or leave the house. It frustrated Kate. Why couldn't her mother just *decide* to be stronger?

It was complicated, Kate realized. Her mother's depression and anxiety were real, not just in her head, and they had changed her. She could only hope that with time, her mother would get better. And that the same thing didn't happen to her brother.

After the recipe was done and Grandma went upstairs to read with Kerry, Kate propped up pillows on the living room couch and settled in to do homework. By ten P.M., she had finished most of it. She plugged her cell phone in to charge and took a shower. While drying off, she heard the wind pick up. The rain came harder, with heavy drops hitting the windows. It felt good to be in pajamas, curled up on the couch again to read. Kate pulled out her copy of *To Kill a Mockingbird* and opened to chapter one. Soon she was immersed in a sleepy Southern town, with children who didn't have a mother and who called their lawyer father Atticus.

Suddenly the lights blinked twice and the house was plunged into darkness. J.T.'s heavy footsteps pounded down the front stairs.

"Power's out!" he said, coming through the living room with a flashlight. "I hope the generator kicks on."

J.T. wasn't talking about a generator for the house, but the generator for the chicken houses. Because none of the windows in the buildings opened, the birds were totally dependent on air-conditioning to stay cool. If the temperature rose too fast, hundreds of birds would start dying. The cost to the Tylers could be huge.

"Do you need help?" Kate asked, following her brother into the kitchen.

"I'll come get you if I do," he said, pulling on a raincoat.

Kate stood at the door as thunder clapped and watched J.T.'s bouncing light disappear through the rain toward the chicken houses. Twice he was silhouetted by lightning in the distance. Within a few minutes, Kate's grandmother—and then her mother—were standing close behind her as they peered through the curtain and waited.

"I'm going to go help him," Kate decided, unable to just stand in the kitchen and wait. After pulling on boots and a raincoat, she grabbed her cell phone and a flashlight, and darted out into the rain.

Approaching the still-darkened chicken houses, she heard a loud engine start up. From out of the darkness, J.T. rounded a corner on the small John Deere tractor, its front light illuminating the ground before it. Kate jumped out of the way and watched J.T. drive in front of the first chicken house, where he backed up.

"J.T.!" Kate hollered above the tractor noise.

"Kate!" he yelled back, surprised to see her. "Hey! Can you hold the light on the hookup? I'm going to try to get the generator going with the PTO! I saw Dad do it once!"

The Power Take Off (the PTO) behind the tractor provided electricity to power the equipment pulled by the tractor. Kate had never thought of using it on the generator that ran the air conditioner, but why not?

"Okay!" she called out. As she took up her position, the wind blew the hood on her raincoat back, and rain pelted her from all sides. Soon, Kate's hair and pajama bottoms were completely soaked.

"Shine the light right here!" J.T. directed.

Kate focused the flashlight, but within seconds, it cut off, probably because the batteries were dead. Stuffing the flashlight in one pocket, she pulled her cell phone from the other. Quickly, she pressed the flashlight app and shielded the phone from the rain with both hands.

J.T. went to work in the splotchy, soft light, trying again and again to get the generator going. Finally, he made a connection. The generator roared to life and, once again, the air conditioner blew cool air into the chicken houses.

"Thanks, Kate! Go ahead inside! I'm going to stay and make sure the power stays on. I may have to gas up the tractor again."

"Of all nights!" she shouted back.

J.T. threw up his hands like, *what can you do?* He smiled. "Tell Mom I have it under control!"

But Kate didn't have to, because her mother was standing right behind them with a thermos in her hands. "Hot chocolate," she said, handing the thermos to Kate.

For a moment, they simply stared at each other while the tractor rumbled behind them. Had Mom really come down from the house?

"Thank you!" their mother said as loudly as she could. "Uncle Ray called to see if we needed help. I'll tell him you have us covered!"

Kate watched her brother grin and nod. "Thanks, Mom," he said, although they were barely able to hear him.

"No," her mother replied. "Thank *you*." Then she pulled her coat tight, popped open an umbrella, and hustled back up the hill to the house.

With power restored to the air conditioner, Kate and J.T. took turns returning to the house to change into dry clothes. Then they waited together in a small room just inside one of the chicken houses where controls for the air-conditioning and heating were located. Shovels and rakes were lined up against one wall with buckets stacked nearby, and long ago, someone had moved in the old card table and a couple of metal folding chairs where Kate and J.T. sat down to begin the long wait.

Toward midnight, a large tractor-trailer truck with several workers arrived to collect the chickens. By then, the storm had blown itself out and, in the lingering drizzle, J.T. went out to greet the driver. While the men pulled on work gloves, Kate and J.T. stepped back. Soon the noisy, messy work began. The birds seemed to know what was up, and right away squawking and feathers filled the air. The men used nets to separate groups of chickens, then grabbed the birds by their feet—four in one hand, three in the other, saving one finger to spring the latch on the metal cages where the chickens were placed.

Hours passed. When the power came back on, J.T. turned off the tractor, but it was still too noisy to talk, so they played cards and hangman, and sometimes rested with their heads on the table. Just as dawn was breaking, the men finished catching the birds and stacked the metal cages on the back of the truck.

"That's it. See you in a couple months," the driver said. Like the other workers, he was slick with sweat and covered with dirt and dust.

J.T. signed off on some paperwork, and the big rig rolled down the driveway with its cargo of caged chickens. Wind ruffled the chickens' white feathers as Kate thought sadly about how they were leaving the only life they had ever known: seven weeks in a darkened chicken house.

"Let's lock up and go to bed," J.T. said, glancing at his watch. "We can probably get a whole hour of sleep before school."

An hour of sleep sounded good. Kate locked up the second chicken house and did a quick check, peering inside the long, empty building. The floor was littered with white feathers— and in a far corner, movement caught her eye.

"J.T.!" she called out the door. "They missed some chickens in here!"

When her brother returned, they slowly approached the three frightened birds. "What are we going to do?" Kate asked.

"Call the company, I guess. Tell them they missed a few."

"But they'll just come back and kill them," Kate said.

"No," J.T. told her. "They'll ask *me* to kill them."

"Well, don't!" Kate exclaimed. "Let them live!"

"Are you crazy? It's against the company's rules to keep any of these birds! You know what the contract says. We can't have another bird on our property! Remember when you found that owl with the broken wing?"

Kate frowned. "I wouldn't have kept him. He needed that rehab place."

J.T. looked skeptical. "You were dying to keep that owl."

"Come on," Kate begged. "I'll be responsible for feeding them, I promise." Her mind scrambled. "We could hide them at Mr. Beck's place next door! No one lives there anymore—and he's got chicken coops in the back."

J.T. tilted his head sideways. "What? Trespass?"

"Who's going to care?" Kate argued.

"Probably no one," J.T. said. He paused. "They won't live long anyway."

"How do you know?"

"Look how fat they are. They're bred to be broilers. They grow way too fast. Why do you think so many of them flip and die?"

Kate's eyes widened. "That's why? Because they grow too fast?"

"Sure it is. Their internal organs grow so fast some of them have heart attacks and keel over. You would, too, if you couldn't move and all you did was eat all day."

Honestly, Kate hadn't known why so many birds flipped.

"And what about food?" J.T. asked. "The company keeps tabs on the feed."

"So we'll buy some feed!"

J.T. still looked doubtful, but there was a slight upturn at the corner of his mouth. "Kate," he said, "you have got to make peace with the food chain."

Quickly, they caught the three birds and placed them in a metal cage that had been left behind. They filled a can with water, scooped feed out of the trough and headed off through the soybean fields to the abandoned Beck property next door. After squeezing through a barbed-wire fence and passing the cage over it, they stepped through the tall grass and weeds behind the farmhouse.

"I'll bet there're a few million ticks in here!" Kate said.

"Yeah, we'll probably be covered with 'em!"

Kate was glad they both wore jeans and sneakers, but she knew the ticks—and chiggers, too—would have a feast on their bare ankles.

The barn at Beck's farm had been torn down years ago. All that was left was a house swallowed by ivy and kudzu and several run-down outbuildings where the farmer used to keep pigs and chickens. They found the old chicken coops, one of which was in fairly good shape, and took the chickens inside. Only one perch was up, but Kate doubted the birds would even know how to fly up and sit on the rail.

"I'll come over after school tomorrow and nail a couple of loose boards in to make it more secure," J.T. said. "And I can probably fix them up a little outdoor run with leftover chicken wire."

"Won't that be something? Except for the walk over here, these chickens have never been outside! They've never seen daylight!" Excited, Kate kneeled on the dirt floor and opened the wire cage. Cautiously, the three chickens emerged.

J.T. stood back and crossed his arms. "I can't believe we're doing this."

"Don't worry," Kate told him. "It'll be our secret." She pressed her lips together. She was good at keeping secrets.

Back at home, changing up for school, Kate heard a text message land on her phone.

Jess: OMG—there's a Facebook page of a chicken with J.T.'s face.

Holding her breath, Kate clicked on the link and saw for herself how J.T.'s eighth-grade picture had been pasted onto a chicken's body. The page was called "Chicken Man." Already dozens of kids had "liked" it. She knew Curtis was behind it. Curtis and Hooper Delaney, who was a computer geek like her brother.

Kate sank down on the edge of her bed. Poor J.T. He did not deserve this. She had to do something. The bully's words repeated in her head: *If you write that assignment for me, I'll leave your wimpy brother alone.*

How could she do that, though? It was cheating!

But wasn't keeping those chickens alive cheating the chicken company?

Wasn't it cheating on her mother when she lied and got J.T. to her father's funeral?

Yes, but in both cases it was for a good reason and no harm was done.

So, Kate thought to herself, if you had a good reason, and kept it quiet, and no harm was done, it was okay?

She chewed on her bottom lip. No. She wasn't at all sure her reasoning made it right.

But even if it *was* cheating, she thought, if you made a deal and kept it quiet in order to protect your brother, to give him a chance and save your family, was it so terribly wrong?

~12~
A GOOD BROTHER

"Come on, Kate! Be aggressive!" the coach yelled.

But Kate froze with the hard, white ball nestled against her field hockey stick.

"Kate!" Coach Dietrich ran along the sideline toward her. "Sometimes a good defense means being aggressive! Go for it! You're wide open!"

Had the coach really said that? It was like she knew what Kate was thinking, only it wasn't about field hockey strategy.

Suddenly, a wing from the opposing team charged full steam toward Kate. At the last instant, Kate calmly flicked the ball over her opponent's stick, then took off and drove it to her left halfback.

"Good job!" Jess said after the game as the two girls walked across the field back to the locker room. "You, like, really faked that girl out!"

"Thanks," Kate said. "Think Coach will let me play sweeper again?"

"Are you kidding? She'd be crazy not to let you!"

"I hope you're right."

"So what happened with J.T. and the Facebook thing?" Jess asked as they continued walking.

There it was again. Everybody focused on J.T. and how he was being bullied. Everyone *seeing* it and *talking* about it—but nobody *stopping* it!

"I don't know if he saw it," Kate said. "He was sick again this morning, so my guess is, yeah, he did see it."

"Gosh, Kate."

"I know, but what can I do?"

"Actually," Jess said, "I was thinking we could organize a protest at school. A whole bunch of kids could get together and make a different Facebook page to support him. I read about this girl who got bullied at her school, and some kids did that, and she was voted homecoming queen!"

Kate was shaking her head even before Jess finished. "There are too many mixed feelings about J.T. right now. It wouldn't work."

Jess sighed as they continued walking. "Maybe pray about it, then. It's all I can think of, to keep praying, and maybe if J.T. ignores Curtis, he'll stop."

Kate turned to her friend. "J.T. has not exactly been egging him on."

A car horn blared from the nearby student parking lot, distracting them, and the two girls stopped.

"What? Is that *him*?" Jess asked. "Is that Curtis Jenkins waving at us?"

"Appears that way," Kate said as her stomach began to knot up.

"What's he doing here after school? Detention probably," Jess said, answering her own question.

This was her chance, Kate thought, staring in his direction.

"What *is* his problem?" Jess continued. "Isn't it enough he bullies J.T.? Don't let him start with *you*, Kate!"

"Don't worry, I won't," Kate said. "In fact, I'm going to go tell him that right now."

"What?"

"I'm going to go talk to him. But let me do this alone, okay?"

"Kate!"

"I'll be right back. I'm just going to talk to him."

"I'm not moving from here!" Jess called after Kate. "I'm *watching*! If he lifts one finger to hurt you, I'm going to have the whole team *and* the coach over there!"

Kate walked quickly, but Curtis had started his truck and was backing out of his parking space.

Breaking into a run, Kate headed for the school driveway to cut him off. She stood boldly in the middle of the road, holding up her left hand to stop him. When he did, she tightened the grip on her field hockey stick and approached the open window on the driver's side.

Curtis seemed amused. "I like your little pigtails, Kate."

Kate glared at him.

"You ain't gonna hit me with that, are you?" he asked, eyeing the hockey stick.

Kate's hard expression didn't change. She actually wondered how many of his teeth she could break with a hard, fast whap.

His grin disappeared. "Uh, Kate, what—"

"I'll do it!" she snapped, cutting him off.

Curtis pulled back. "What? Hit me?"

Kate's heart was already pounding from two hours of exercise and a run across the field, but now it beat triple time. "I'll write that essay for you if you leave J.T. alone. And if you take down that Facebook page *immediately*!"

"Aha," Curtis said. He relaxed and the smirk reappeared. "All right, then. Good decision. It's a deal! And I'll get that computer problem fixed ASAP."

"So give me your cell phone number."

"You want my number? Cool!" Curtis replied.

"Not because I *want* it, but I'll need some information if I'm going to write that assignment for you."

"Oh, yeah, right." Curtis rooted around in his truck for something to write on and ended up giving Kate his cell phone number on the back of a gas receipt.

Kate snatched it from his hand and ran back across the field.

"Thanks!" Curtis called after her. "You won't be sorry!"

But Kate didn't know if she'd be sorry or not. This was new territory for her—*cheating*. It was a gamble that came with a high price, because her good grades, her reputation, all of it was at stake if anyone found out.

But what could she do? No one else was stepping in to help her brother. Kate bit her lip so hard she actually drew blood.

"What did you tell him?" Jess asked after jogging to meet Kate.

"I told him to leave J.T. alone," Kate said, balling up her hand to hide the slip of paper.

Jess snorted. "What? You think he's going to listen to you?"

Kate didn't want to say much more. "I think he'll be nicer," she told Jess. "I told him I just wanted to be friends, that God was watching—and I think we connected."

Jess's eyes grew big.

Kate couldn't help herself. "Yeah, I was thinking of Proverbs. How about 'a gentle answer turns away wrath: but a harsh word stirs up anger.'"

Now she was not only a liar *and* a cheater, but a blasphemer, too, Kate thought. She pressed her lips together and could taste the blood from her lip.

Jess beamed. "Kate, that is awesome! I mean, that is so incredibly awesome."

"Well," Kate said, licking her bottom lip as they resumed walking, "we'll see about that."

After dinner, after a trip to check on her refugee chickens and homework, Kate went to fetch Hoppy from his cage outside and took him up to her room. She closed the door and let the rabbit explore while she sat cross-legged on her bed and sent the first text message to Curtis.

Kate: A short bio. So tell me about urself.

Curtis answered right away.

Curtis: What do u want to know?

Kate: What do u like to do? Other than bully people?

Curtis: Wrong attitude . . .

Kate: What? U think I enjoy this?

No response. Had she insulted him? She needed to be careful.

Kate: How old are u?

Curtis: 16

Kate: Tell me about ur family.

Curtis: Like what?

Kate held her hands palm up and asked her stuffed panda, "Do you believe this?"

Kate: Who do u live with?

Curtis: My mom and her boyfriend.

His mother's boyfriend. She wondered what happened to his father.

Kate: What do u do outside of school?

(She mouthed, silently: "Besides be mean to people?")

Curtis: Not much. Weekends I work at this bbq place.

Okay, what else? Kate wondered. She thought of the camo clothes he wore.

Kate: U hunt?

Curtis: No.

Kate rolled her eyes. Was that all he was going to say? But then another text came.

Curtis: Fish. Me and my brother, justin, we fished every river and creek in the bay.

Kate: No way. My uncle is a waterman. Over a hundred thousand creeks and rivers flow into the bay. No way u fished every one.

Curtis: Maybe not all.

Another long pause. While she waited, Hoppy tried to jump up on Kate's bed, but couldn't quite do it without the missing hind leg. Kate reached down and scooped him up. When he settled beside her, she stroked the cottontail between his ears and watched as he closed his eyes. Kate glanced back at her silent phone. She wasn't going to get any information from Curtis if she kept insulting him. She sent another text.

Kate: *What do u fish for?*

Curtis: *Sun, perch, trout but mostly rock. First time I fished with my brother i caught a 32 inch rock weighed 16 lbs.*

Kate: *How old were u then?*

Curtis: *6 or 7. Got a picture of me holding that fish on my bureau.*

Kate: *To catch rock, what do u use for bait?*

Curtis: *I like live-lining with small spot and circle hooks.*

Kate had no idea what that was, but fishing, yes, that would be the topic of the short bio she'd write for Curtis.

Kate: *How old is Justin?*

No response. Kate waited a minute or so before texting again.

Kate: *How old is ur brother?*

Curtis: *Justin is 8 years older than me.*

Kate: *Are u close?*

Curtis: *Very.*

Kate: *What makes him such a good brother?*

Curtis: *My brother was tough and no one ever messed with him. Smart too and we had a lot of fun.*

Kate: *Like what?*

Curtis: *Fishing and camping mostly. My brother taught me everything I know about engines.*

Kate was trying to think of the next question when another text came:

Curtis: My brother looked out for me when nobody else did.

Kate: Guess u'd do just about anything for ur brother, right?

Curtis: U name it.

Kate: Interesting because I have an older brother I love a whole lot, too. And look what I'm doing for him.

~13~
TOO LATE

K ate lay in bed listening to the rain beat on the tin roof and cascade noisily down the metal gutters. She didn't think she'd ever get to sleep. But then the cat jumped on her bed, startling her, and Kate sat up with a start, afraid Hoppy was still in the room. But no, she had taken the bunny back to its cage late, before turning out the light. So she must have fallen asleep. The digital clock glowed the time: 4:30 A.M. Something heavy weighed on her mind: the texting with Curtis. Instantly, Kate was wide awake.

It had been a mistake to cut him off and throw those notes in the wastebasket, hadn't it?

But was it too late?

She had an hour and a half until she needed to get ready for school. There was still time.

Kate threw off the covers and stepped carefully through the early morning darkness to her small desk where she turned on her computer. Quietly, she pulled the wastebasket from beneath her desk and plucked out the two pieces of lined notebook paper she'd balled up. They crinkled as she smoothed them out on her lap.

First, she went online and researched fishing in the Chesapeake Bay. She skimmed several articles, highlighted portions, then cut and pasted them into a separate Word document. She scribbled notes on a pad of paper beside the keyboard. When soft morning light started to seep in through the blinds at her window, she started writing. *"Fishing for Striped Bass in the Bay," by Curtis Jenkins*, she began. *This is a book that every fisherman should have . . .*

By six A.M. she had the 250 words she needed. Quickly, she took a shower and dressed for school by pulling on jeans and the first clean top she came across. After combing out her wet hair, she pulled it into a ponytail bun, popped gold studs into her pierced ears, and gently slid the newly printed assignment into her backpack.

"Good Morning, Sea Hawks! I'm Karen Duvall for WCOR at Corsica High School. Today is Thursday, September 5. Hot lunch today is chicken egg roll or hot ham and cheese sandwich. The grill line is spicy chicken tenders . . ."

Listening to the morning announcements, Kate realized she hadn't made herself a sandwich, and she'd been planning to avoid the cafeteria. She didn't want to talk to anyone that day, not even Jess. She just wanted to hide out, get the paper to Curtis, and be done with it.

"Auditions for the fall performance of *No, No, Nanette* will be held tomorrow after school. Tickets to the homecoming dance will go on sale next Friday . . ."

How could she even think about things like the homecoming dance? Who would ask her to go, anyway? There was only one boy at school she liked, but forget that. It didn't matter, Kate tried to tell herself. Dances, pep rallies, football games—they were for the other kids. Already, she circulated in another realm at high school, an outside one.

The announcements continued. "Just a reminder that the county fair opens in two and a half weeks. . . . A high of seventy-five degrees is expected today. . . . Now here is Jessica Jones with the Quote of the Day. Take it away, Jess!"

Kate pressed her lips together, hoping Jess wasn't about to commit social suicide.

"Good morning, Sea Hawks. I found this quote online. Yeah. I don't know who it's from, but I thought it was good. Here goes: *When something bad happens, you have three choices. You can either let it define you. Let it destroy you. Or you can let it strengthen you.* I hope you'll think about it. Have a nice day!"

Not bad. Kate grinned. Good for Jess! Kate thought back on the quote and wondered if what she was about to do would define her, destroy her—or strengthen her. For sure, she didn't think the cheating would make her stronger. But the whole point, Kate decided, was to make J.T. stronger, to give *him* a chance, not her.

Again, she unzipped her backpack and felt inside with her hand to be sure the writing assignment she'd done for Curtis was where she could grab it quickly.

*

Creative Writing was after the lunch break. Kate lingered in the hallway just down from the classroom door, waiting and watching for Curtis. When she spotted his camo shirt and blond hair, she walked swiftly in his direction.

"What's this?" he asked, looking at the folded piece of paper Kate quietly offered.

"What do you mean, *what's this*?" she whispered harshly.

Curtis pushed her hand away. "I don't know. You really ticked me off last night, Kate, so, like, I don't think it's gonna work."

Kate swallowed hard. She pressed the paper against the books in her arms and hoped no one was watching. There was a pause. It flashed through her mind that there was still time to *not do it*.

"Will you leave J.T. alone?" she asked.

"Maybe." Curtis shrugged. "Maybe not. Guess it depends on how I feel."

What a jerk, Kate thought. *He's never going to stop.*

"Did you do the assignment for writing class?" Kate asked.

He made a funny grunting sound. "No—"

"Then *here*. We had a deal, remember?"

Hurriedly, Kate pushed the paper into Curtis's hand, and this time he accepted it. She looked at him, and their eyes met. "Now leave J.T. alone."

It was done. She had officially cheated. There was no going back.

A funny thing happened next: nothing.

Nothing happened.

For an entire week, nobody bullied J.T. Every day, he went

to school. He completed all his assignments. He cleaned out both chicken houses and hooked up the bucket loader to the John Deere to scrape out several inches of caked chicken manure from the floors. He cut the rhododendron bushes back from around the house. He taught Tucker a new trick, weaving between his feet while he walked, and built an outdoor run for Kate's rabbit. He even dug out his basketball and practiced shooting into the rusty hoop on the back of the tractor shed.

Grandma had left for North Carolina, but Kate's mother was getting up early, cooking meals, cleaning, doing the wash, and helping Kerry with homework. She was making dinner, too. She still didn't drive, however, which forced Kate and J.T. to find rides home when they stayed after school.

Kate was up to her ears in homework every night, largely because field hockey practice and games took up so much time in the afternoon. She had been playing sweeper regularly and liked the new position. She'd also been making regular trips to feed and check on her three refugee chickens, and at school she had attended the first meeting of the newspaper staff, where she'd signed up to write features. And Marc, her lab partner, had followed up on getting those notes from class the day he had to leave early. They'd even met at lunch one day to study for a quiz.

"So who is he?" Jess asked as they changed up for field hockey practice.

"Marc Connors, a boy in my biology class," Kate said.

"He's cute," Jess said.

Kate smiled shyly and finished pulling a T-shirt over her head. "We were just studying for a quiz."

"Uh-huh, uh-huh."

Kate didn't say anything more, but Jess was in a chatty mood.

"Guess what movie I watched last night? *Mr. Popper's Penguins*. Remember that book in second grade?"

Kate grinned. "In homeschool we made lapbooks for it!"

"I loved making those, didn't you? All those pictures and poems we pasted in. I still have the one I did for *Black Beauty*.

Jess finished tying her cleats and scooted down the bench to sit closer to Kate, who stood at the full-length mirror dividing her hair to make pigtails.

"Kate, can I ask you something?"

"Sure." Kate's eyes flicked to her friend's.

"Olivia's having a sleepover Friday night. You won't be mad if I go, will you?"

"Of course not," Kate replied automatically, while ignoring the pinch deep inside. She focused back on herself in the mirror and kept braiding.

"I didn't want to do it behind your back," Jess said.

"Don't be silly."

An awkward moment passed. Jess examined her fingernails while Kate braided.

"Okay, well, thanks," Jess said. "I'll see you outside, okay?"

Kate gathered hair into her hand for the second pigtail. "Yup. I'll be right out."

"Jess!" Kate called suddenly, running after her friend.

Jess turned at the door.

"I just wondered," Kate said, hesitating, still holding one unfinished braid. "Are we still going to the county fair like we always do? Just you and me?"

Jess beamed a reassuring smile. "Of course!" she said before sprinting out the door.

We'll get our friendship back on track, I know we will, Kate wrote in her journal that night. *Just as soon as I can stop worrying about J.T. and what I did for Curtis.* I think about going to Mr. Ellison and confessing but then I know Curtis would just start up again. . . .

As the days went by, Kate had begun to think that the cheating might be completely in the past, when Mr. Ellison decided to read a few of their author note assignments aloud in class.

The first one he chose was written by Jasmine Albright about making beaded jewelry. She called her book *Gems by Jasmine.* The second piece chosen to be read aloud, *Breaking Boards*, was by Jim Tucker, who described working toward a black belt in karate. The third was Kate's: *Treasure Hunting on the River*, by Kathryn Tyler.

"*Ever since she was little*," Mr. Ellison began reading, "*Kate Tyler has loved walking the riverbank to look for sea glass that washes up on the narrow beach. Over the years, she has collected jars full of pieces large and small in all colors of the rainbow. Miss Tyler says, "'It's amazing how, over time, an ugly shard of broken glass from a discarded bottle of beer or ginger ale is transformed into a smooth, polished piece of sea glass.'*"

After he finished reading, Mr. Ellison noted Kate's word choices: *shard* instead of *piece*, and *transformed* instead of *made*. "Make every word count," he said. Kate felt her cheeks flush with pride and embarrassment. But there wasn't time to bask in the praise. The next assignment Mr. Ellison chose to read aloud was *Fishing for Striped Bass in the Bay*, by Curtis Jenkins.

Why was that piece the next one? Kate's stomach clenched. Did he suspect something? Kate couldn't help glancing across the room. She watched Curtis stretch his eyes like he was waking up from a nap and sit up from his slouched position.

"*This is a book that every fisherman should have on the shelf or in the tackle box,*" Mr. Ellison read aloud. "*A lifelong resident of the Eastern Shore, sixteen-year-old Jenkins has been fishing the bay's rivers and creeks ever since he was five. 'My brother taught me everything I know about fishing,' he said. 'First time out in Pope's Creek, I snagged a thirty-two-inch rockfish that weighed a hefty sixteen pounds.'*"

Kate took shallow breaths. The phrase, "a cold sweat" popped into her mind. She worried that Mr. Ellison had recognized her writing. It felt like every word read aloud was another blow— another nail pounded into the coffin of her reputation. She was a cheater. It felt like a portion of her soul had died.

"*This book offers tips on when and where to find Maryland's striped bass, noting that the fish love the deep shipping channels of the bay,*" Mr. Ellison continued. "*Although most anglers are happy reeling in a twenty-to-thirty-pound rockfish, Jenkins says it's not unheard of to catch a trophy rockfish upwards of one hundred pounds in the Chesapeake Bay. This is Jenkins's first book.*"

"So! What do we learn about Curtis from this piece?" Mr. Ellison asked.

A hand went up. "That he really loves fishing," a boy said.

"But is that a reason you'd want to buy this book?" the teacher probed.

A girl this time. "No, but the book is full of tips and advice."

"What pulls us into this piece? What did we talk about last week?" Mr. Ellison asked the class.

"Specifics," a student told him. "He started out by saying the first time he ever fished was with his brother in Pope's Creek."

"Good!" Mr. Ellison responded. "This piece also tells me that Curtis Jenkins is a pretty good writer. When he walked into class last week and said he was here because there was no place else for him to go, I had my doubts. But not anymore."

Kate had stopped breathing. Was Mr. Ellison being sarcastic because he knew the truth?

Everyone in class was turning to look at Curtis, who sat tall, smirking, with his arms crossed tightly across his chest.

"Writing comes from a deep well inside each of us," Mr. Ellison said. "You can learn a lot about yourself by writing."

For sure, Kate thought. She had learned a lot about herself by writing. Specifically, that her writing had made her a cheater. It was real. There was no going back. She wasn't a perfect student anymore.

When class was over, Kate was the first person out the door.

"Kate!" she heard Curtis call in the hallway. "Wait!"

But Kate was not waiting or stepping aside for Curtis Jenkins this time. She plowed her way through the crowd at the doors and practically ran down the stairs.

~14~
CONFLICTED

Saturday morning, Kerry sat at the kitchen table eating a warm oatmeal muffin and, with sticky fingers, arranging piles of plastic beads according to color and size. She was still in pajamas, with two long braids, fuzzy and rumpled from sleep, falling forward over her shoulders.

"Not right now," Kate warned as she reached across the table with a damp cloth and wiped off the breakfast crumbs. "I said after I get my chores done, remember?"

Kerry continued sorting.

"Did you hear me? Hey, and don't get crumbs all over, Kerry. I just cleaned there!" She put Kerry's muffin on a plate and wiped the plastic tablecloth a second time. Then she started the dishwasher and wrapped up half a dozen muffins in tinfoil, a small gift for Jess's mom, who was taking her food shopping later. Kate's job again, since Grandma was away for a while.

It had been two weeks since Kate wrote the paper for Curtis, and several days since Mr. Ellison read it in class. The weekend's arrival was a relief. Yet still, there was a sharp edge to the way Kate felt, a tight feeling in the pit of her stomach. After wiping off the table, she wrung out the dish cloth a second time because she couldn't remember if she'd done it the first time and draped it over the edge of the dish drainer.

"If anyone needs me, I'll be down at the tractor shed," J.T. said as he came through the kitchen.

Kate watched him put on his Orioles cap and walk out. She grabbed a carrot and a chunk of lettuce from the refrigerator and tapped Kerry on the head. "I'll be back in a few minutes, okay? I need to feed Hoppy." But what she really wanted to do was find out how school was going for J.T. Was Curtis leaving him alone? Was there at least some payoff for what she had done?

Kate found her brother in the tractor shed standing on a wooden crate so he could pop open the engine lid on the big John Deere. After peering inside, he pulled out a mouse nest from behind the battery and flung it behind him making Kate jump.

"Sorry! Didn't see you!" J.T. apologized. "This tractor hasn't been driven in over a year. It's no wonder the mice moved in. Hey, Kate, while you're here, would you give me the grease gun?"

Kate retrieved the tool from a shelf behind her and handed it to her brother.

"Miss Hatcher is coming this morning," J.T. said as he started squirting grease on the tractor's joints. "She wanted to take us bowling, but I told her I didn't think we'd have time."

"Bowling?" Kate crossed her arms. "Your probation officer is taking you bowling?"

"*Us*, Kate. She wanted you to go, too. Duckpins though, on account of her little girl would have to come, too."

"I have to do the food shopping," Kate said.

"Yeah, and I've got the new chicks arriving." J.T. stepped off the crate and kneeled to reach the lower tractor joints. "I'll tell her another time."

"Another time, for sure," Kate agreed. "It would be fun. Could we invite Jess, too?" she asked, not forgetting that the sleepover at Olivia's was last night.

"Sure," J.T. said.

Kate leaned against the wall and watched J.T. work. "So, how are things going at school?" she asked after a while.

"Okay," J.T. replied. He seemed pretty upbeat. "Did I ever tell you what I'm doing for my science club project?"

"No," Kate said. "What is it?"

J.T. stood and picked up the crate with one hand so he could move to the other side of the tractor.

Kate uncrossed her arms and followed.

"I'm going to try to see what's in that poultry feed by testing the chicken manure," J.T. said, stepping back up on the crate. "Our science club adviser, Mr. Stanley, says we might be able to use labs at the community college."

Kate loved seeing J.T.'s old enthusiasm. "So how are you getting that manure?" And then it hit her. "Hey! Are you sneaking onto other farms at night to get samples?"

J.T. stopped greasing the tractor and looked down at her.

"Can you keep something between us, Kate?"

"Of course," she said.

He stepped down off the crate. "Sneaking onto other farms at night is *exactly* what I've been doing."

"That's where you've been going at night?"

J.T. nodded.

Kate almost laughed with relief. "I thought it was drugs!"

"Drugs?"

"Yeah, that little Baggie of stuff."

"You saw that? That was chicken manure!"

When J.T. started to laugh, so did Kate. "Before that, I thought maybe you were out there exercising or something to get in shape."

"For *what*?"

"I don't know! To fight, maybe. Fight Curtis."

J.T. rolled his eyes. "Oh, wow. Man, I wouldn't do that, Kate. If I got into a fistfight, I'd get sent back to Cliffside."

"I know! That's why I worried!" Kate exclaimed. "But stealing manure. I mean, couldn't that get you in trouble, too? Or get those farmers in trouble?"

"No, I'm not identifying the farms."

"Are you looking for arsenic?"

"What? You knew?"

"You told me about it once, remember? You said arsenic was in the feed bags Dad used to cut open."

"Oh, yeah, I did. Well, that's the big one, for sure," J.T. confirmed. "I mean, they're not supposed to put that stuff in the feed anymore, but I wanted to check." He stepped back up on the crate so he could go back to greasing the tractor joints.

Kate moved closer and crossed her arms. "Okay, here's what I don't get," she said. "If chickens get fed arsenic, then how come they don't get sick and die?"

"Because it's not poison when it's in the feed," J.T. said as he worked.

When J.T. saw Kate frown, he paused and came down off the crate once again. "Look," he said. "There are two kinds of arsenic—organic and inorganic. Organic arsenic occurs naturally. It's in the soil; it's in our water. The kind of arsenic they might put in chicken feed is organic. They put it in the feed to kill a parasite that may or may not be in the chicken's gut. But in the chicken's body, the *organic* arsenic changes into *inorganic* arsenic."

"It *changes*?"

"Yes! It turns into the kind of inorganic arsenic that's bad, that can cause cancer. Plus, because it's in the chicken, it not only ends up in their meat, but in their manure, which is used on fields to grow vegetables! Then, when it rains, all that chicken manure gets washed into our streams, where it can affect the fish!"

Kate was astonished. "It affects the fish, too?"

"Yeah. What do you think Dad and Uncle Ray always argued about? Mostly runoff from the chicken manure. Dad's business was affecting Uncle Ray's. The watermen and the chicken farmers, they're always fighting. But their whole ways of living are at stake."

Perplexed, Kate pressed her fingertips to her temples. "So if Maryland and other states already ban arsenic from the feed, why are you looking for it?"

"I just want to check," J.T. said. "From what I read, no one's testing for it. Wouldn't it be something if I found some? Or something else? Maybe even something worse?"

Kate crossed her arms again. "I still don't understand, not totally, but it sounds important. I just hope you don't get us all in trouble."

"Don't worry, I won't. But don't tell Mom or Uncle Ray, okay? I don't want them to freak out. Hey, and by the way, my manure samples are in the freezer."

"Yuck! You put chicken manure in our freezer?"

"No big deal. It's under that frozen lasagna."

Kate made a face. "Yeah. Well, I'll try not to use it for dinner one night."

J.T. snorted and went back to work while Kate started toward the house.

"Kate, wait!" J.T. called after her. She stopped and turned.

J.T. came to the door of the shed with the grease gun in his hand. "I just wanted to thank you. I mean, I never did tell you how much I appreciated you getting the trumpet out to me so I could play at Dad's funeral."

Kate started to smile. "You're welcome."

Just then, a huge flock of honking Canada geese flew close overhead, moving toward the cornfield across the street. As the flock's shadow passed over, Kate and J.T. leaned their heads back to watch and listen as the air was stirred by hundreds of wings. It was an awesome sound. Kate loved it when the geese came. There was something reassuring and hopeful about their arrival. J.T. grinned and seemed to be thinking the same thing.

An arriving text message interrupted her thoughts.

"Gotta get going. See you up at the house," Kate said as she pulled out her phone.

Curtis: I need to talk to u. ☺

What? A message from Curtis with a smiley face?

Kate: STAY OUT OF MY LIFE!

Angrily, Kate shoved the phone back in her pocket, but it dinged again.

Curtis: Don't have to yell. Since u don't want to talk, the new assignment is what role did the nile river play in early civilization? 2 pages doublespace due tuesday.

Kate's eyes grew large with disbelief. She texted back so fast her fingers hit all the wrong letters and she had to delete everything and start over.

Kate: No! Our deal is done.

Curtis: U stop u know what happens.

Fuming with anger, Kate marched up the hill and stomped into the kitchen where Kerry looked up expectantly. "Are you ready now?"

Kate's shoulders slumped. "I can't, Kerry. Not now!"

"You said!"

"I know I did, but something's come up."

"But we were going to make a necklace!"

"Kerry, please—"

"You promised!" Kerry wailed.

"All right!" Kate held up both hands. "But just *one*, okay?"

Kerry's face showed instant relief. "First, you have to pick a color."

Kate surveyed the piles of beads, but what she was really trying to decide was whether or not she needed to deal with this new assignment from Curtis. If she didn't, would the bullying start again? Would things get worse? Just when they were getting better for J.T.!

She felt trapped. *What's the word for this?* she wondered, staring over Kerry's head. *Blackmail? Extortion?* She would have the text message to prove it! But then she'd be in trouble, too. And would that really help J.T.?

"How come you're mad?" Kerry asked.

Kate shook her head. "I'm not mad."

"Then how come you're standing up, and you're not smiling, and you're not talking?"

"I'm sorry," Kate said, putting a hand over her eyes. "I guess I'm tired."

"But we just got up!"

Kate took her hand away and suddenly felt sorry for Kerry, who had been waiting so patiently for her. "How about blue?"

"Okay!"

When the necklace making was over, Kate rushed to her bedroom and closed the door. She reread the text. *The new assignment is what role did the nile river play in early civilization? 2 pages doublespace due tuesday.*

What was she going to do?

She sat on the edge of her bed and stared at the floor. She got up and paced the room. She lay on her bed and looked out the window. She even folded her hands in prayer. But no clear answer appeared.

Her eyes fell upon the pile of books on her desk. Kate was not a cheater. She was an honest person who worked hard and got straight A's. She needed those grades so she could get a scholarship and go to college and make her mother proud.

She chewed on her lip and decided to ignore Curtis Jenkins. If he texted again, she wouldn't read it.

Her phone dinged again. Kate couldn't help but glance at it. This time the message was from Jess: *"I know what I'm going to be for Halloween!"* No reference to the sleepover. Did she think Kate had forgotten?

She set her phone aside and sat at her desk, frustrated about what to do, then flipped open her assignment notebook to scan the work that was due: twenty problems in math and three pages of dialog in Chinese. A chapter in biology and preparation for the lab they would start on Tuesday studying the effect of acid rain on the germination of seeds. Kate needed to buy dried beans and paper towels for the experiment. She texted her lab partner, Marc, reminding him to bring Ziploc bags and stick-on labels. Then she made two notes: *questions for the newspaper interview with Mr. Ellison* and *pack a clean uniform for the field hockey game.*

Kate's day of homework was interrupted only when her mother gave her the food list and asked her to go to the grocery store with Aunt Helen because something had come up for Jess's mom. Once again, Kate didn't see anyone else her age with a list and her own cart at the store. At least she knew the aisles by heart and could do it quickly: produce first, then tuna and canned goods, then cereal, then dish detergent, then cat and dog food, then milk and bread.

In the meat section, she paused. Her friends always thought it was strange that Kate and her family raised chickens but if they wanted to eat one, they had to buy it at the grocery store. No one understood how they didn't actually own the chickens they raised. She held a package of chicken breasts in her hand, noticing how pink and plump the meat, how it glistened underneath the plastic wrap. What did J.T. say? Burst blood vessels? Chicken was on the list, but Kate set the package back and decided that for one meal this week, they could do soup and grilled-cheese sandwiches.

All day the text message from Curtis followed her. In late afternoon, she closed the door to her bedroom again. No thoughts of Curtis in here, she told herself. Grabbing her school journal from the nightstand, she plopped onto her bed and leaned against her pillows.

What my room says about me:

You can tell the minute you walk into my room that I love pandas because on the wall over my desk is a poster of the panda named Tai Shan who was born at the National Zoo in Washington, DC. Tai Shan means "peaceful mountain." After Tai Shan was born, we checked the zoo's Giant PandaCam every day. We watched Tai Shan grow from the size of a butter stick to a toddler panda who curled up in a bucket for a nap and played with a soccer ball.

Kate stopped writing. Thoughts of Tai Shan didn't end happily, because the panda cub belonged to China, which took him back a few years later. Kate had cried watching his plane leave on the evening news.

She didn't understand why the Chinese cared so much about pandas but didn't seem to care about what was happening to the elephants. Kate had read an article online and seen a special program on television that said the Chinese love for ivory statues and trinkets was one of biggest reasons so many elephants were being killed—so their tusks could be sold on a black market. Sometimes whole herds of elephants were wiped out so poachers could hack off their tusks. Just thinking about it made Kate's eyes go bleary with tears. Someday, she was going to help stop this. It was the reason she was taking Chinese in high school. Someone needed to explain it to them! Someday she would have a job in which she could help protect beautiful and endangered animals like elephants and pandas. *Someday*.

Kate wiped at her eyes. She didn't write this down, but she had often wondered if her love for animals wasn't because of the tortured feelings she had about what her family did for a living. She knew she was "conflicted." Her third-grade Sunday school teacher had told her so when Kate blurted out in class once how she hated the way her family made its living.

Below the panda poster was a sparkly frame holding a photograph of Jess and Kate, each carrying a candle, the night they were inducted into the Junior National Honor Society. Kate knew if anyone ever found out about the cheating, she'd be asked to leave the honor group.

The other framed photo on Kate's bureau was of J.T. and his friends Brady and Digger. They were eight or nine years old and stood by the steam locomotive they rode for Brady's birthday. The boys were laughing and had their arms around one another's shoulders; Digger was making rabbit ears behind J.T.'s head. The world was wide open. Not so long ago, those boys had had dreams, too. . . .

Kate pulled out her cell phone: *U stop u know what happens*.

~15~
SPECIAL DELIVERY

Kate! Wake up!" A hand shook Kate's shoulder. Was it the middle of the night? Kate blinked her eyes open in the dim light.

"I didn't mean to scare you," her mother whispered.

"Mom!" Kate pushed herself up on one elbow. "What is it?"

"I'm not sure," she said. "I walked out to get the morning paper."

Kate sat all the way up. "You walked all the way down the driveway?"

"Shhhh!" Her mother was not smiling. "Yes. I did."

"But, Mom, that's great!"

Her mother was shaking her head. "No, because I saw that someone has smashed down our mailbox. It's on the side of the road!"

"They did?"

Her mother leaned closer. "There was chicken manure and feathers stuffed in the box."

Kate gasped and put a hand up to her mouth.

"They left this note," her mother said, handing Kate a piece of paper.

The note, written in black marker, read *Special Delivery for the Chicken Man, aka the Baby Killer*.

Kate was horrified. Chicken Man was bad enough, but *Baby Killer*?

"Do you know what this means?" Kate's mother asked, her frightened eyes glued to Kate's.

Kate took her hand from her mouth and started to move her head back and forth. "No—"

"Kate, what's going on?"

Kate's eyes moved away from her mother's. Her head stopped moving.

"Chicken Man," her mother said. "Isn't that what the boy in middle school called J.T.?"

Kate couldn't deny it. She nodded.

"Is this the same boy, then?"

"I don't know," Kate said, unsure how to answer. She met her mother's eyes again. "Maybe."

"There's something you're not telling me."

The pain on her mother's face was clear. It was a bad situation, no question about it. But Kate was glad to see that her mother cared.

"Is it Curtis Jenkins?"

Her mother had remembered his name!

Kate swallowed hard. She didn't want her mother to get depressed again. "It's probably just kids fooling around," she hastened to say. "Really, Mom, you shouldn't worry." She pushed her covers aside. "I'll go clean it up now so he won't see."

"We'll both go," her mother said.

Pulling a sweatshirt on over her pajamas, Kate stepped into flip-flops and followed her mother downstairs. It was not yet seven o'clock, and everyone else was sleeping. At the back kitchen door, both Tucker and Jingles squeezed through and rushed ahead of them. Outside, the sky was clear; it promised to be a sunny, crisp day. Hundreds of geese were already eating in the nearby cornfields.

"Get a garbage bag and a shovel from the garage," Kate's mother directed her. "I'll get some work gloves and a hammer."

They must have looked odd, Kate thought, as they set off down the driveway, Kate in pajamas, Mom still in a robe, her long hair gathered into a loose braid, and the dog trotting alongside them.

When they got to the mailbox, Kate pulled on the work gloves and, with her mother holding the garbage bag open, kneeled to scoop up handfuls of chicken manure and feathers.

Sickening . . . despicable . . . hateful. These were some of the words that came to mind as Kate worked. Had Curtis driven over during the night and smashed it down? With what? A baseball bat? A sledgehammer? It seemed like a cruel and violent thing to do.

While Kate tied up the garbage bag, her mother dug out the old posthole. It took some effort, but the two of them managed to get the post back in and the mailbox up. Kate shoveled in dirt around the base and stomped on it. The mailbox still had a big dent, but at least it could hold mail.

"I'll ask Uncle Ray to get a new one at the hardware store,"

Kate's mother said. "Maybe he can put it up sometime this week."

"We'll definitely need a new one."

"We won't say anything to your brother," Mom added.

"No," Kate agreed. "We won't say anything."

As far as she could tell, J.T. never did find out about the mailbox, but the episode was far from over. The next day at school, Kate was summoned to the office at the end of second period. She was surprised to see her mother standing at the front counter. She wore a green corduroy skirt, one she used to wear to church, a freshly pressed blouse, and a shawl. Her hair was pulled back into a tight bun, and she clutched her big black pocketbook, the one that looked like a saddlebag.

"Mom, what are you doing here?"

"I came to talk with Mr. Roberts."

"The assistant principal?"

"Yes." Kate's mother motioned for Kate to follow. "Let's go out into the hall."

Kate looked around. What was going on?

In the hall, Mom led her toward the front doors and then stepped to one side. "We had a talk, in Mr. Roberts's office. I told him what happened to our mailbox. I showed him the note. I said we knew who did it." Her eyes began filling with tears.

"Mom?" Kate touched her mother's arm.

"Mr. Roberts says there is nothing school can do about it. They can't do anything about an incident that happens off school grounds."

Kate nodded, although she already knew this.

"At least now the principal's office is on notice to keep a look-out for Curtis doing something here," her mother said.

"Wow, Mom. I didn't think you'd actually come to school."

"I want to help him, Kate."

"I know you do. I do, too!"

Her mother shook her head. She rummaged in her giant purse for a tissue. "I've been an awful mother. That poor boy has needed my help for so long, and I've let him down. I've been so neglectful. So wrong."

"He knows you love him, Mom," Kate said, trying to comfort her.

"I don't know what to do," she said, dabbing at her eyes.

Outside, a white taxicab was pulling up to the curb.

"Oh, gosh. That's for me," Kate's mother said, sniffing, balling up the tissue. "I need to get home. We'll talk again later, okay? We'll think of something, Kate. There has to be a way we can help him."

Kate hugged her mother and watched her walk out to the cab. It was *huge* that her mother had called a taxi and come all the way to school. Kate hadn't even known there were taxicabs available out in the country! Where had it come from? Chestertown? Easton? It must have cost a lot of money. Money they didn't have. But Grandma wasn't here, and she knew Mom didn't want to ask anyone else to drive her.

As she stood at the window watching her mother, Kate's heart broke and her own eyes misted over. Once again, she thought back to the day they had buried her father, how J.T. had been on the knoll with his trumpet, and nobody ever found out about it. And the first paper she'd written for Curtis? Mr.

Ellison had never caught on. So it was possible, after all. You *could* keep a secret if you were careful.

Standing at the window watching the taxi drive off, Kate took a deep breath. There was only one way she could think of to help J.T. and her mother. She needed to research and write a paper on the Nile River's role in early civilization. Two pages. Doublespaced. Due tomorrow.

~16~
BACKSPIN

They agreed to meet before school at the water fountain on the second floor. That end of the building, near the chemistry labs, didn't have lockers or homerooms. Neither Curtis nor Kate thought anyone would see them there.

Curtis was waiting. He leaned against the wall, but straightened up when he saw her.

"Here," she said, thrusting forward the paper she'd written on the Nile River.

"Thanks," he muttered, quickly folding the paper and slipping it inside the math book in his hands.

Wasn't he even going to look at it? To be sure it was two pages? Or that it had a separate cover sheet with his name on it as he'd requested in a subsequent text?

"That's it," Kate declared. "No more." She turned to go.

"Wait," he said. "I just wanted to ask you something. For our Creative Writing class—"

Kate swung all the way around. "No!"

Curtis threw up his hands. "I'm not asking you to write it!"

Kate stared at him.

"I just wondered, can you help me get *started* with it?"

"What? The describe-your-room piece?"

Curtis nodded.

Too bad he was such a creep, Kate thought. With a haircut, he could actually be sort of cute.

"Look," he said, opening his hands. "I just don't know where to start."

Kate glanced at her watch. They had ten minutes before first period. She could ignore him. Just turn and go, which was what she wanted to do. Or she could stay for five minutes and be nice. Maybe some of her nice would wear off on him.

"Like, how do you do it?" he asked again.

Was this for real? Kate wasn't sure. "Just dive into it," she said with a slight shrug, still unsure of his motive. "Try something, and if that doesn't work, try something else."

Curtis stared at her expectantly.

"Like, where *is* your room?" she suggested. "Do you share it with—"

"It's in the basement," Curtis told her.

"The basement," Kate repeated.

"Yeah. I have the basement to myself."

"Okay. Well, is it nice and cozy down there?"

Curtis smirked. "It's really damp, for one thing."

"Eww," Kate sympathized, although she couldn't care less if Curtis Jenkins was uncomfortable in his own bedroom.

"No, I like it! I mean it's damp, but it's also cool—as in *not hot*—and I hate being hot. So all the time I hear the sump pump running 'cause the groundwater, it comes in through a pipe in the walls and gets pumped back out into the yard. We're on a really low piece of land, so it's, like, running all the time."

"That must be pretty annoying," Kate said.

"Actually, I kind of like it," Curtis said. "It drowns out everything going on upstairs. You know, like the TV blasting away and my mother yelling at her boyfriend."

Curtis laughed, but Kate didn't think it was funny. She couldn't imagine what it must be like having a mother with a boyfriend, never mind a mother who *yelled* at her boyfriend. Kate's parents had had disagreements, but she could think of only a couple times when they'd actually raised their voices at each other.

There was a lull in their conversation, and Curtis kicked at the floor with the toe of one sneaker.

"Write down what you just told me, Curtis. 'I sleep in a damp, cold basement, but I like it'—and then explain why."

"Okay!" His eyebrows arched. "I'll try that. I will."

What in the world was happening? Kate wondered. "You may want to include some other details," she added. "Like what does it smell like in the basement? Is it messy? Do you have a TV down there?"

"No TV," Curtis jumped in to say. "But there's a pool table! Yeah! My brother, Justin, and me, we played a lot of pool. He taught me how to backspin the ball. Do you know what that is?"

Kate shook her head.

"That's when you hit the cue ball with the cue stick at the base of the ball. It makes the ball move forward, but when it hits another ball, it suddenly reverses direction and comes back."

"It hits and then comes back?" Kate asked.

"Yeah. It's really amazing!"

"Interesting," she said, thinking to herself that the whole meeting with Curtis was like a giant backspin. What was it with him?

She tried to think of some more questions. "So when you lie in bed, what else do you see besides the pool table? Pipes in the ceiling? What's on the walls?"

"My fishing rods," he said. "I got all my fishing rods lined up on the wall. Then, on my bureau there's a picture of my brother and me when I caught that thirty-two-inch rockfish. Remember I told you about that? And there's a picture of Justin when he graduated from basic training." He paused, and his eyes fell away from hers. "I look at that picture every night before I go to sleep."

His brother again. There was something about his brother.

And then suddenly, Hooper Delaney was there. Silently, and without a greeting of any kind, he stood a few feet behind Curtis, like a shadow, and leaned against the wall. He was half the size of Curtis, a short, skinny kid who wore glasses and a large, dark sweatshirt with the hood up so Kate couldn't see his face very well. His hands were stuffed into his pockets, and he didn't have a backpack or anything. Kate couldn't be sure, but he seemed to be *leering* at them. Did he know what was going on? Had Curtis told him they were going to meet here?

Curtis glanced at him over his shoulder. "Hey, Hoop," he said flatly.

Hooper didn't respond.

It was creepy, Kate thought. Hooper was really sketchy.

Didn't he have anything better to do than hang out and cheer on the bully? When he started biting on a fingernail, Kate began to wonder if there was something wrong with him.

And then, the strangest thing happened: Curtis's demeanor began to change. He crossed his arms and frowned like he was angry. "So anyway, Kate," he said, his voice suddenly loud. "Your next assignment is for English."

Was this a joke? Because it seemed like he was playacting. He had gone from laughing and asking for her advice to asking her to cheat again? Was he serious? Or was he showing off for Hooper? Kate was confused.

"I know you must've read *Animal Farm* in eighth grade like everyone else," Curtis said, "so this shouldn't be too hard for you."

He was serious. Kate started walking backward.

"But some of us dummies are just now reading that book."

Kate turned and started running down the stairs.

"It won't be that hard! I'll text you the assignment!" Curtis called out over the second floor railing.

Kate went so fast that on the last step, she fell, scraping her knee. It wasn't a bad cut, not really, but she'd hit the edge of the step, and it drew blood, giving Kate an excuse to head for the nurse's office. When she got there, she said she'd fallen and didn't feel good. The nurse led her into the back room, where she pushed aside a curtain revealing a bed.

All morning, Kate hid out, curled up on the bed in the sickroom. She even stayed through lunch, letting the nurse bring her a tuna fish sandwich and some cold French fries on a tray. Would Jess miss her at their table?

Poor Jess, Kate thought, so innocent, chattering away on the bus that morning about the Halloween costume she was going to make, not knowing what Kate was about to do. And Kate not responding at all because she was still miffed about the sleepover. *Kate, did you get my text? I'm going to be a cupcake! I saw a picture in this magazine at the orthodontist yesterday. It's really cool. You use, like, cardboard for the cupcake paper, right? Then you stuff white tights with rags and loop them around and around for frosting. And you glue on cut-up colored straws for sprinkles! Kate? Are you even listening . . . ?*

Kate put a hand over her eyes. She was going to lose her best friend in all this, too. Things were slipping away, because what about the interview with Mr. Ellison for the school newspaper?

"Excuse me, but could you get a message to one of my teachers?" Kate asked the nurse in a panic. "I'm supposed to interview him at lunch, but there's no way I can do it." She grimaced. All those questions for nothing: *Where are you from? Where did you go to college? Do you like to write, too?* She had agonized over the personal stuff, uncertain whether it was rude to ask if he was married and had a family.

"Sure," the nurse said.

"Oh!" Kate sat up and rummaged in her backpack pulling out a roll of paper towels and a bag of beans. "Can you take these to the office, too? My lab partner, Marc Connors, needs them for lab. Mr. Rutkowski's biology class next period."

The nurse took the items but hesitated and gave Kate a second look. Did she suspect Kate was faking it? She moaned a little and lay back down.

What about field hockey? she wondered, draping a hand over her eyes. Could she go to practice if she hadn't been in class all day?

The nurse sounded concerned. "Are your cramps usually this bad? Should I call your mother?"

Yet another lie added to her heap of lies. The pile was getting so big Kate couldn't see over the top. "No," she replied. "My mom doesn't drive, so she can't come. I'll be okay. The Aleve will help, I know it will."

~17~
A MONSTER

*D*ust and the smell of hay as we walk across fields turned into
   parking lots.

Merry-go-round music. Kids screaming on the baby roller coaster.

A man with tattoos on both arms hands us tickets.

The sweet aroma of cinnamon roasted nuts.

*A woman in a wheelchair face paints a flower on the cheek of a
little girl.*

Man on stilts—so tall he wears a hat with a basketball hoop.

*Red, white, and blue ice cream—pink cotton candy—red candy
apples.*

The sun burns into our scalps. We should have worn hats!

A sign for camel rides.

Kate and Jess looked at each other. "Camel rides?"

"You've got to put that in your notes!" Jess insisted, tapping
the edge of Kate's notebook. "Since when does Maryland have
camels?"

"I want a camel ride!" Kerry exclaimed.

Kate smiled and wrote that down, too.

"How many things do you need?" Jess asked, peering over Kate's shoulder.

"He didn't say how many. He just said use your five senses to describe the county fair."

"Fun," Jess said. "I wish I'd taken Creative Writing."

"I do! I want a camel ride!" Kerry whined.

Kate rolled her eyes at Jess. "I hope this wasn't a mistake," she said behind her hand to Jess. The afternoon with Jess was important to Kate. She had looked forward to the fair all week. Taking Kerry along had been Mom's request at the last minute when Jess's mother drove into the yard. But no one had had the heart to say no, not even Kate.

"Don't worry about it," Jess said. "She'll be fine. We'll have fun."

Kate didn't say anything, but she noticed how Jess not only had mascara on, but a shimmery blue color on her eyelids, too. It was actually kind of pretty, Kate thought. It brought out Jess's bright blue eyes.

She turned back to her little sister. "Let's walk around first and see some stuff. Then we'll get tickets, and you can ride the camel, okay?"

The girls walked past a hot tub display and then a booth where the spicy smell of sizzling peppers, onions, and Italian sausages filled the air. But in the exhibit hall, endless rows of preserved tomatoes, pickles, and jams got boring really fast.

"Kerry, come see the honeybees," Kate said.

"Ewwwww! Will they sting us?" Kerry asked.

Jess snorted. "Well, maybe, if you break open the glass and stick your hand in there!"

Kerry pressed her nose against the display glass. "What are they doing?"

"They're making honey," Jess said, kneeling down to explain. She was always so good with Kerry, Kate thought. Probably because she didn't have a little sister or brother of her own. Jess even remembered Kerry's birthday every year and always brought her a bunch of balloons—all different colors, which Kerry adored and held onto for weeks, long after they'd lost all their helium and languished on the floor.

Glad to be free for another minute, Kate moved on to the next display and took more notes: hand-knit sweaters, a beautifully carved walking stick. Quickly, she surveyed the flower arrangements until a single, giant pink zinnia caught her eyes. Instantly, it reminded Kate of a lotus blossom . . .

The ancient Egyptians said the Nile River's delta looked like a lotus blossom, because of the way the water seasonally overflowed its banks and fanned out before it emptied into the Mediterranean Sea. When the river flooded, then withdrew, it left thick layers of silt that enriched the land.

Kate had researched the paper on the Nile River in the library last Monday on her lunch break. The Egyptians became excellent farmers, who irrigated their land and trained oxen to pull a wooden plow. . . . She had written it up that night and printed it out before she even started her own homework. They grew fields of wheat and other grains. . . . She had been up for hours after she finished that paper for Curtis because she'd had an essay to write for English, two chapters to outline in American history, and a math quiz coming up.

Her mother had tapped on the door at midnight.

"Kate," she said, poking her head inside the door, "you need to get some sleep."

It was nice that her mother cared, Kate had thought, even if she didn't know why Kate was up so late.

"I will, Mom. I'm just finishing." But it was another hour before Kate darkened the room at one A.M., and even then she hadn't studied the math.

"Kate? What *is* it?" Jess rushed over. "Are you okay?"

"Yeah. I'm fine," Kate said, not even realizing she'd put a hand on her chest and was leaning forward as the flashback washed over her. "I was just thinking."

"Geez, I thought you had a stomachache. It looked like you were going to throw up!"

"I want to go to the rides!" Kerry insisted, jumping up and down.

"I'm okay," Kate assured Jess. "Let's take her to the rides."

As the three girls walked between food stalls toward the midway, Kate forced herself to take more notes.

"Look, three kinds of funnel cake now!" Jess exclaimed. "Chocolate, pumpkin, and glazed! We'll have to try all three for your sense of taste!"

After they bought tickets and put Kerry on the merry-go-round, Jess put her hands on Kate's shoulders and turned her around.

"Okay, Kate Tyler. Look at me. You need to tell me what's wrong. What is going on?"

"What do you mean, 'what's wrong'?"

"Just what I said. You've been on another planet! I mean, I see you on the bus. I see you in math. I see you at field hockey. But it's either too noisy or there's never time to talk. And you don't eat lunch with us anymore!"

Kate was caught off guard and unsure how to respond.

"Don't go telling me it's worry over J.T.," Jess said, "because I see him almost every day in the cafeteria now, and he's always eating with either Steven O'Connell or that girl Ashley. So what is it? You even missed field hockey practice, and you *never* miss practice!"

Kate dropped her eyes. "I had a lot to do," she mumbled.

"A lot to do? Like *what*?"

"Like homework!" she shot back, starting to get annoyed that Jess wasn't backing off.

"Everyone on the team has homework!"

"I know, Jess, but I had a lot. And I didn't have study hall because I had to make up the bio lab I missed."

"Yeah, and I know you didn't pass that last geometry quiz. What's with that? We could have studied together."

Kate looked away and didn't answer.

"Kate, you're *different*."

"Well, so are you," Kate argued. "I mean, you didn't used to wear all that makeup and stuff."

Jess pulled back and seemed hurt. "We're in high school," she said softly. "All the other girls are wearing makeup."

"Not *all*," Kate countered.

"No, not all," Jess said, shrugging slightly. "I just wanted to try it. It was Olivia's idea. But anyway, what's so wrong with trying some mascara and eye shadow?"

Nothing. Nothing was wrong with putting on a little make-up. Kate hated herself for what she'd just said. Truth be known, she wanted to try some, too! But she didn't know how or when to try it. And she didn't have the money. Kate sighed and dropped her head. She wished she could tell Jess that in addition to her own homework and field hockey and all her chores at home last week, she'd had to go on a hunt for her copy of *Animal Farm* (thank goodness she found it in J.T.'s room). Then she'd had to reread the first six chapters so she could write a summary, all in one night. Not only that, but two days later, she'd had to create a timeline on ancient Egypt as well as write an essay describing the social pyramid that placed the pharaoh on top and the slaves at the bottom. An essay, no kidding, that made *her* feel like a slave!

But Kate couldn't confide any of that, so the two of them stood there, silent, not knowing what to say, until Kerry came running back and grabbed one of Jess's hands and one of Kate's and, walking backward, pulled them toward the food. Jess bought a warm pumpkin funnel cake covered in confectioners' sugar that came on a paper plate. The three of them pulled it apart and ate it in small, messy bites. When they finished, they cleaned their sticky hands and wiped their mouths with napkins dribbled with bottled water. Then more rides: the Tilt-A-Whirl twice, and, for Kerry, the whirling teacups, which almost made Kate sick for real. Surprisingly, however, things actually seemed a little better.

After the midway, they walked through the petting zoo, where aggressive, hungry goats bleated for handouts and an angry llama laid its ears back and looked like it was ready to spit. Kate gazed at three little pigs in the pen and couldn't help seeing them all with names like Snowball, Napoleon, and Squealer—the pigs in *Animal Farm*. She imagined them taking over the petting zoo and revolting against the owner, who kept them in tiny enclosures and ferried them from fair to fair.

"Whoa! Look at me!" Kerry called out from atop the camel's hump. She sat in a specially designed seat that had low rails to grab for safety.

"Hold on!" Jess told her.

"Five dollars for a three-minute ride," Kate grumbled after using the last of her cash to pay for Kerry's ride. But she and Jess took pictures with their smartphones and joked about the camel's whiskers and its long, beautiful eyelashes. Suddenly it hit Kate. What was this camel doing in Maryland? What kind of a life was it having, traveling to small-town carnivals and giving rides?

She should have been outraged about the camel. She and Jess both! But there were other issues now—and a wall between them: Jess wondering why Kate had changed, and Kate unable to tell her.

As they left, walking back through the exhibits and food stalls, they paused to watch a man use a chain saw to sculpt a blue heron from a log.

"Oh, my gosh, look!" Jess said. "Isn't that Curtis Jenkins?"

Kate squinted and stared. It was Curtis, all right. Behind the chain-saw artist and the haze of flying wood chips was the back of a food tent, and Curtis, wearing a white apron, was hauling out bags of trash.

"Looks like he's working hard," Jess said.

"Curtis Jenkins is a *monster*," Kate blurted.

"Oh, come on!" Jess said, pushing her arm playfully. "He's not a bully anymore."

It was hard for Kate not to respond.

"My mom said he had a really hard time after his brother died," Jess said. "Maybe he was angry about it. Maybe that's what made him so mean."

"What did you say? When his brother died?"

"Don't you remember? His brother was that army guy who came to talk to us in the fifth grade. He told us what it was like being a soldier in Afghanistan."

"I remember the soldier," Kate said. "We wrote letters and sent his unit a big Christmas package, right? But I didn't know that was Curtis's brother."

"Yeah, it was. My mother said he died, like, the next year or something. We prayed for him at church."

Kate was slowly shaking her head. "Why don't I remember that?"

"Maybe that was the same time your dad got sick."

"But even if Curtis was angry about what happened to his brother, it didn't give him the right to bully *my* brother!"

"No, it didn't," Jess agreed. "But that's over, isn't it? You told me yourself that things were fine."

Kate couldn't deny that.

"Honestly, I don't know what's got into you," Jess went on. "You didn't use to hold a grudge like this. And anyway, Kate, just remember this—inside every monster there's a human being."

Kate rolled her eyes. "Maybe you should make that one of your quotes!"

"Yeah! Well, maybe I will!" Jess said, spinning away.

~18~
DISTRACTION

*C*ould Jess be right? Could there be a human being inside the monster that was Curtis Jenkins?

Kate pondered this question the next day in English class while Mrs. Langley collected homework.

Why was Curtis making her write all these papers about ancient Egypt and *Animal Farm* and yet, when she quietly slipped these assignments into his hands, he didn't look at her and seemed almost *embarrassed*?

"Books closed. Eyes up here," Mrs. Langley instructed.

But Kate turned to look out the window instead.

She thought back to the time she had talked to Curtis about his room in the basement and his brother, Justin. She recalled his description of the funny-sounding lures he used in fishing and how he explained the backspin in pool. Why did he seem so normal then? Why did he change when Hooper showed up?

A light rain was starting to hit the classroom windows. Kate wondered: If she was nicer to Curtis, if she talked to him more and got to know him better, would it make a difference?

The rain came harder, and Kate narrowed her eyes, thinking. Jess was on her mind, too. She needed to talk to Jess and clear the air—

"Miss Tyler!" Mrs. Langley's voice rang out. "Is the view out that window distracting you?"

Kate swung her head around. "No, ma'am."

"Then tell us, Miss Tyler, how you would sum up chapter five?"

Kate swallowed hard. Her mouth went dry, and her heart beat fast. She hadn't been listening. "Chapter five," she repeated, scrambling while her mind reeled backward. She had finished the book last night. There were only ten chapters in the book, so chapter five was about halfway.

"Yes, chapter five," Mrs. Langley confirmed.

"Umm. This is the chapter," Kate began slowly—she'd have to take a chance. "The chapter where Squealer makes the incredible statement that all animals are created equal. But then he goes on to say that the animals might not make the right decisions, so they should trust Napoleon to make the decisions for them. This is so hypocritical, because if all animals were created equal, then Napoleon could make a mistake just as easily as *they* could."

Mrs. Langley was frowning. "And remind us. Who is Napoleon?"

"The pig who takes over," Kate replied.

"And what book are you referring to?"

Kate felt her insides drop and the blood rush to her face. "*Animal Farm*," she murmured so softly it was almost a whisper.

She was talking about *Animal Farm*, not *To Kill a Mockingbird*, which is what her class was reading. "I'm sorry."

"Yes. I think we need to have a chat," Mrs. Langley said, peering over her reading glasses at Kate. "After school, Miss Tyler."

Kate pressed her lips together and blinked her eyes, holding in the tears. She pushed her back against the chair and entwined her hands together tightly in her lap. She was so embarrassed. *So. Incredibly. Embarrassed.* Was somebody going to figure out now what she'd been doing? Had she just given herself away?

At lunch, Kate wanted to hide out in the library, but she stood bravely at the edge of the huge cafeteria, her eyes desperately scanning the crowd for Jess.

"Hey!" Kate said, approaching her friend from behind.

Jess turned and acknowledged Kate with a quiet "Hey."

"Can I sit with you guys?" Kate asked, noting that Olivia was already at the table setting down her tray, and that Samantha and Lindsey were there, too.

Jess shrugged. "Sure," she said, pulling out a chair.

"Kate, you should get hot lunch today. It's Walking Taco," Olivia piped up.

"Yeah, your old favorite," Jess said.

True. Walking Taco had been Kate's favorite lunch at middle school. A bag of Doritos on a tray with hamburger meat, salsa, and cheese. What you did was dump the meat and other things into the bag and shake it up. You could eat straight from the bag if you were in a rush. Or, you could sit down and eat it with a fork. But Kate didn't eat meat anymore, and Jess knew that—so why did she say that?

Kate was not going to give up. She wanted Jess to know she was sorry. She pulled out the chair beside her friend and rummaged in her backpack for the granola bar she'd brought.

Lindsey was wrapping an apple core in a napkin. "Hey, Jess," she said, "can I have one of those Rice Krispie treats you brought?"

Jess's eyebrows went up. "No! They're for the game this afternoon."

"Please," Lindsey begged. "I'm *starving*."

But Jess shook her head. And Kate wondered if she'd remembered to pack a clean uniform and her green and yellow ribbons for the game.

"What's your quote for tomorrow morning?" Samantha asked.

Jess seemed pleased by the interest—but was Kate the only one noticing a silly smile on Samantha's face?

Leaning to one side, Jess pulled a pink index card from the front pocket of her backpack. "I was trying to find something about forgiveness," she said after she retrieved the card.

Kate cringed a little, assuming that comment was directed at her.

"I wanted a quote about how everybody needs to let go of negative things and move on," Jess said. "But I'm not sure I found the right thing."

If Jess only knew the whole truth, Kate thought, as, slowly, she broke off a tiny piece of her granola bar and slipped it into her mouth. She honestly wondered right then if it would be easier to *not* have any friends for a while.

"I don't know," Jess said, focused on the quote. "Maybe I need to rethink this one."

Olivia snatched the card out of Jess's hands and put up an elbow to keep Jess from taking it back. "*If you can't live through adversity,*" she began reading aloud, "*you'll never be good at what you do. You have to live through the unfair things, and you have to develop the hide to not let it bother you and keep your eyes focused on what you have to do.* Maurice 'Hank' Greenberg."

For sure it seemed thought-provoking, Kate thought, especially the last part: *keep your eyes focused on what you have to do.*

Jess grabbed it back, and for a moment, no one spoke or offered an opinion.

"See, I'm just worried it doesn't have anything about forgiveness in it," Jess said to break the silence.

If Jess was so hung up on forgiveness, then why wasn't she forgiving Kate for their argument at the fair? Why was she acting like she was still mad?

"Well, I think it's dorky," Olivia declared. "You're going to embarrass yourself, Jess."

"I agree," Lindsey chimed in. "It's too long. You ought to just do short and funny. Can I have one of your chips, Olivia?"

Samantha lifted her chin and scrunched up her nose. "And anyway, who's Hank Greenberg?"

After the final bell that day, Kate rushed to the upstairs hallway, where she saw Curtis waiting. Discreetly, she passed him the paper, complete with a separate title page and Curtis's name, about how *Animal Farm* was an allegory, using specific examples from the story. It wasn't a very difficult assignment, because Kate had remembered how the animals' rebellion against their farmer was supposed to represent the Bolshevik revolution against the Russian czars. The interesting thing that Kate remembered most about the book was how the animals slowly turned into the thing they had rebelled against.

Curtis took the assignment, rolled it up, and held it in one hand. Would he even read it? She *hated* what she was doing.

"I got in trouble today in English," she said bitterly.

"For what?" Curtis asked. "Being smarter than everybody else?"

"Very funny," Kate responded with a straight face. "I got confused about which book we were reading because of the paper I just wrote for *you*."

"Oh." Curtis dropped the smart-aleck grin. "Sorry that happened."

"Really?" Kate couldn't help herself. "How sorry are you, Curtis?"

He looked away. "So I tried to write something about the county fair last night," he said. "For Creative Writing—"

"We saw you at the fair," Kate said quickly. She didn't want him to have time to even think about giving her another assignment.

"You did?"

"My friend Jess and I, we saw you hauling trash behind the food tent."

"Oh," Curtis said, dropping his head and looking a bit embarrassed. Maybe he didn't want people to know.

"Seems like you could have gathered a lot of details from your job," Kate said.

Curtis gazed skyward. "Use your five senses, right? Okay. Well, about the only thing I *heard* all day was that guy's chain saw. The guy making birds and bears out of wood? As for *smell*? Three smells. When I was inside the tent, it was burgers and grease. When I was outside dumping trash, it was wood chips. There was so much sawdust in the air I was coughing by the end of the afternoon.

"What did I *see*? Not much other than that black, smoking grill. I burned myself three times." He stuck out his arm so she could see the pink, blistered skin.

"I worked all day without a break," he went on. "So all I *felt* was tired. Tired and hungry 'cause I was supposed to get, like, fifteen minutes to eat, but it never happened, so I didn't *taste* anything neither. Get this—when a homeless guy showed up at the back and asked if there was anything in the trash he could have, I gave him a burger on a roll and told him to beat it, quick."

The words had come in a rush. When he finished, he ran a hand through his hair.

"Wow. You could write a really good piece, Curtis," Kate said quietly.

"What? You think that's interesting?"

"Of course it is. Most kids don't have a clue what it's like to have to work hard like that."

"I have to work. Every weekend I work for that guy at his barbecue place. Got to keep up the truck on my own—gas and everything. Nobody helps me with that. And my truck—that's my freedom. I can get away from things in my truck."

"Maybe you could write about how you felt working when other kids your age were walking around eating funnel cake and corn dogs," Kate suggested.

Curtis shoved his free hand into the other pocket of his jeans. He was struggling with something. When she averted her eyes, she saw the pile of books he had set on the floor.

"Why do you have *Huckleberry Finn*?" she asked. "I thought you were reading *Animal Farm*."

Curtis straightened up. "We are," he said. "This is what we're reading next."

Kate had a sinking feeling. She hadn't read Huck Finn.

"It's the first novel to ever be written entirely in dialect," Curtis said.

But Kate wasn't interested in hearing about it. "I need to go."

Suddenly, Curtis pulled his hand from a pocket of his jeans and held out a small piece of paper. "Look, I hate doing this."

Kate backed away. "Then *stop*!"

"I can't," Curtis said.

"Why not?" Kate demanded.

"You don't understand."

"No, I don't! Why can't you just do your own homework—and leave my brother alone?"

Curtis peered around nervously. Who was he looking for? Hooper?

"Kate, please. It's, like, out of my hands."

She scowled. "What do you mean, it's *out of your hands*?"

"I can't explain it right now. I'll make this assignment the last one, okay? I promise. If you don't do it, J.T. will get hit hard with some bad stuff."

Kate's arms and hands fell limp at her side. What was going on? She didn't understand. But did he just say this would be the last time? She let Curtis lift one of her hands and set the folded paper in her palm. In a very odd gesture, his fingers gently made her fingers curl around it.

They looked at each other, and Kate felt a rush of mixed emotions. Not hatred or anger. Confusion, mostly. Enormous confusion and an incredible yearning to bring the whole thing to a close.

"Do you promise this is the last one?" Kate asked him.

He held her gaze and nodded.

Curtis took his hand away from hers. "Don't you, like, need to go to field hockey or something?"

Kate suddenly remembered the meeting with Mrs. Langley. "Oh, my gosh, yes!" she exclaimed, a hand to her forehead. "But you need to explain this to me, Curtis!"

"I will. I promise."

Kate whirled around. Already late for her meeting with Mrs. Langley, she half ran the rest of the way, her hands on her backpack straps to steady her, her mind spinning. What did Curtis mean when he said she wouldn't understand? So strange, how Curtis's large, rough fingers had closed around her hand. . . .

The session with Mrs. Langley was not as painful as Kate feared. She told her teacher she'd been up late doing homework, and had read *Animal Farm* to help her brother. She figured Mrs.

Langley wouldn't know enough about her brother's schedule to question what English class he had. Yet another lie thrown on the heap. She topped it all off by saying, "I'm so sorry, Mrs. Langley. It was almost a year ago today my father died. I guess I was distracted."

It worked. Mrs. Langley didn't give Kate a detention, just a warning.

Outside the classroom, Kate closed her eyes for a two-second silent prayer to her father asking him to forgive her for using him as an excuse, then glanced at her watch and took off toward the gym. She was twenty-five minutes late for practice.

"Kate!" a boy's voice called out on the stairwell.

Kate stopped and turned to see her lab partner, Marc.

"Wait up, Kate. There's something I want to ask you!"

"Marc, I can't! I'm late to field hockey!" She resumed her rush down the stairs. At the bottom, she paused briefly to call back, "Send me a text, okay?"

The locker room was empty by the time Kate arrived to change. Quickly, she pulled on shorts and a T-shirt, threw her things into the locker, and pulled a hair elastic over her wrist. She'd make a ponytail out on the field, since there wasn't time to braid her hair. A mad dash out the back door—and abruptly, Kate stopped. The field was empty. The team wasn't out there, because they had an away game today. The bus had already left.

Kate sank down on the cement steps leading to the athletic fields and held the field hockey stick across her lap. She hadn't even packed her uniform.

Missing the game without an excuse meant she was automatically off the team.

~19~
LIKE A TURTLE

It took nearly an hour and a half for Kate to walk home from the high school. She'd never had to walk home before, and the main highway was nerve-racking, especially when tractor trailers barreled by blowing sand in her eyes. When she was finally off the busy road, the route became quieter—and a lot safer as it wound through the countryside past farms and fields. Along the way, she saw a fox and two deer, and almost stepped on a tiny lizard.

By the time Kate turned up the long driveway to her home, she had thought a lot about her situation. It would be embarrassing to be off the team, and it would hurt, for sure. She could only hope it didn't further damage her friendship with Jess. But there was so much else on her mind that she was almost relieved.

Field hockey wasn't the only thing to go. Because she hadn't written the piece on Mr. Ellison for the school newspaper, she had stopped attending newspaper staff meetings. And poor

Marc, her lab partner. What did he want? She'd probably never know now. He hadn't sent a text and probably never would, because she'd been so rude by not stopping to talk. Probably just as well, she thought. She didn't have time for a boyfriend or a social life.

Getting good grades and protecting J.T. were the two most important things, she decided. There was always next year for the newspaper and field hockey. In the spring, she could try out for lacrosse—or maybe softball. Things would be settled down by then. Now if she could just come home after school every day, she'd have more time for homework and chores—and that one last assignment for Curtis. She felt the piece of paper in her pocket: *Compare and contrast hieroglyphics and cuneiform.* She'd have to do some research for that one.

As she neared the house, Kate could see her brother walking off toward the tractor sheds. And then, as she got closer, she noticed the family van parked in a different spot—off to the left under the maple tree near the old swing set, instead of to the right where it usually sat in front of the garage. Soon she was able to see that someone was sitting in the driver's seat. Not J.T., but her mother?

What was that all about? Kate crouched behind the tangle of forsythia that lined the driveway and crept closer. Had her mother driven the van from one side of the yard to the other? She was trying, wasn't she? She was doing battle with her demons, whatever they were. Not wanting to interfere, Kate stayed low behind the bushes and circled the yard, sneaking in the back door of the house.

After changing into jeans and a long-sleeved T-shirt, Kate

set aside her cell phone, picked up her personal journal and a pen, and quietly slipped back outside. She planned to take care of her chickens next door and then sit outside their coop and write. But first she wanted to check in with her brother.

"What happened?" Kate asked, finding J.T. in the tractor shed standing with one hand on his hip and the other drumming his fingers with annoyance on the tractor's fender.

"That darn choke. I flooded the engine, so now I've got to wait for some of the gas to evaporate before I can try again. A complete waste of time."

"No," Kate said. "I mean with Mom? Why is she sitting in the van?"

J.T. shifted his attention to Kate. "She's still there?"

"Yeah. Just sitting."

"I don't know. I mean, she drove the van down the driveway and met me at the bus and let me drive back. I thought she got out after I did."

"She *drove* the van?"

"Wonders never cease, huh? She was just letting me practice so I can go for my learner's permit in a couple months."

Kate returned to the doorway and looked up the hill again toward the maple tree where the van was parked. She knew it had taken a huge effort on her mother's part to not only get in the van again, but to take it down the driveway.

"So what are you going to do?" Kate asked, noticing that J.T. had attached the big mower, the Bush Hog, to the back of the large red tractor.

"They're getting ready to harvest the soybeans. Uncle Ray hired someone. But before they come, I want to trim the brush out of the field that got left fallow last year. If I don't, we'll have a forest out there."

"Well, watch out for turtles," Kate said.

"What?" J.T. screwed up his face. "You looking for another injured animal to take care of?"

"No! Don't you remember how Dad used to stop the tractor if he came across a turtle? He'd get down to move it."

"Oh, yeah!" J.T. brightened. "Right! And he had to be careful when he set the turtle back down, to keep it headed in the same direction."

"Yes! Because turtles only go in one direction! If he put the turtle down on the wrong side, the turtle would simply walk right back into his path."

J.T. smiled. "Huh. I haven't thought of that in a long time."

Talking about their dad made them both grow quiet. When Kate sat down on a pile of old lumber, J.T. took a seat beside her and hunched over with his elbows on his knees.

"I miss Dad," he said.

"Me too."

"I never realized before how much talking we did out here while we worked and fixed stuff. I learned a lot from him."

Kate nodded.

"He sure loved going to my basketball games, didn't he?" It was more of a statement than a question.

Kate readily agreed. "He did. He loved watching you play."

"I was thinking I might go out for the team this winter."

"That would be great!"

"But we'll see. I'm not sure yet," J.T. said. "I really want to get this project done first. Boy, and I'll tell you, if Dad was here right now, he'd be mighty interested in what I'm doing."

"Did you find out yet if your chicken manure samples have arsenic?"

"Not yet. We haven't found a lab where we can test them. In the meantime, I'm doing some other research. You know what I found out?"

"What?"

"Some companies add antibiotics to the feed."

"Is that bad?"

"Probably, because the kind of antibiotics they discovered in some chicken samples may keep the chickens from getting sick, but they get passed along in the meat and can create antibiotic-resistant superbugs in people."

"That sounds pretty scary."

"It is! For sure, I'm going to include that in my report."

"Do you think Valley Shore puts that stuff in *our* chicken feed?"

J.T. shrugged. "Who knows? Nobody's testing it. Boy, Valley Shore would go nuts if they knew I was poking around in this stuff."

"But I feel really proud of you, J.T., for doing this. It sounds important. I'm glad you got involved and that you've bounced back at school with everything."

"Well, not *everything*," J.T. disagreed.

"Why?" Kate asked, alarmed that there was a bullying incident she hadn't heard about. "What else happened?"

Her brother made a tent with his fingers, but didn't answer.

"J.T., what is it? You can tell me." Kate nudged him gently with her elbow.

"Well, there's this girl at school."

Surprised, Kate turned to look at him. "Yeah," she said, smiling and feeling relieved it wasn't bullying after all. "Some of us noticed!"

"What? Like, at lunch?"

"Her name's Ashley, right?"

J.T.'s face softened, then flushed. "Ashley Newberg," he confirmed. "We were in band together in middle school. She plays flute in the marching band. She's been trying to get me to join up."

"I remember Ashley," Kate said. "She looked different in middle school, though."

"I'll say! She looks great now, doesn't she? I mean, she lost a lot of weight and let her hair get long."

"Maybe that's why I didn't recognize her at first."

"She wrote to me, you know, when I was at Cliffside."

"She did?"

"A couple times," J.T. said.

"So what's bothering you about Ashley?"

"This guy, he's a junior, he asked Ashley to homecoming."

"What? And *you* wanted to ask her?"

"I don't know. I'm not sure I even want to go."

"If you don't want to go, then what's the problem?"

J.T. pushed the glasses up on his nose. "That's what I'm confused about. She said she didn't give that guy an answer yet."

"She told you that? Then she must be waiting for *you*!"

"I don't know, Kate. I don't know what to do."

Kate smirked. "You dummy. Ask her to go! Why not?"

J.T. stood up and wiped his hands on a rag. "I'll think about it." He climbed up into the tractor seat, pushed in the clutch, gave it some gas, and this time, the tractor sputtered, then roared to life.

Kate got up and moved out of the way. She waved to J.T. and, journal in hand, set off to feed her chickens. As she walked across the soybean field, the plants, turning brown with autumn, brushed against her legs. She heard the old tractor settle into its regular *putt-putt-putt* and, glancing back, saw J.T. sitting tall in the high seat. She smiled, knowing that her brother's mind wasn't solely on chicken manure.

By the time she'd crossed the field, Kate could also hear the loud *chomp-chomp-chomp*—and occasional *zing!*—of the Bush Hog as its powerful blades tore through the tangled brush and every now and then sent a rock flying.

After squeezing through the barbed wire at the edge of the Beck property, she walked up a small incline toward the chicken coop. Her three chickens were just sitting there, as usual. She fed them some grain and refreshed their water from a jug she kept in the corner. Then she sat outside the coop, leaning up against its worn, gray wood in a sunny spot, and opened her journal. She made notes about the entire day, from the humiliation of English class to the surprising sight of her mother sitting in the van, to the revealing conversation with J.T.: *I just hope his testing of the chicken manure samples for arsenic doesn't get our family into trouble.*

She chewed on the end of the pen, and tried to write a conclusion. *Basically, I'm still not sorry for the cheating I've done, be-*

cause it protected J.T. and gave him a chance. I guess I need to be like one of those turtles crossing the field and just keep going in the same direction, no matter what.

The sound of the tractor and the Bush Hog suddenly got louder, distracting Kate. Odd, she thought, because the fallow field J.T. was cutting didn't abut the Beck property. What was he doing way over here?

Kate stood and walked a few steps to where she could get a better look. Shading her eyes with one hand, she stared, suddenly alarmed. The tall, red tractor was rumbling through the soybean field, chewing up the plants about to be harvested, as it circled without direction—and without a driver.

~20~
SO MUCH BLOOD

Dropping her journal and the pen, Kate sprinted to the fence. Had J.T. jumped off the tractor? Had he fallen? Kate's eyes swept the field again. He could have hit his head. He could be lying in the field somewhere, knocked out and hurt!

Unable to see any sign of him, Kate yanked up the top strand of wire, squeezed through, and took off, jumping over the rows of soybeans, as she raced to where J.T. had been cutting.

The tractor, meanwhile, continued its menacing arc. If her brother was lying unconscious in the field, the tractor and the Bush Hog could run over him and shred him into a million pieces! She'd heard her dad tell stories about Bush Hog accidents. No one ever survived an accident with a Bush Hog.

Finally, she could see the path J.T. had cut with his first sweep of the tractor. Her eyes followed the cut area until she saw how the tractor must have crossed one of the field's drainage ditches. At that point, the path deviated and went off at an odd angle. Suddenly, a spot of blue caught her attention—J.T.'s shirt! Her brother lay in the brush beside the ditch.

"J.T.!" Kate screamed, rushing to his side.

Blood was everywhere—on her brother, on the grass beside him. There was even a gruesome red trail along the path the Bush Hog had cleared. Stunned, Kate pressed her hands to her face and dropped to her knees beside him. "J.T.! I'm here!" She squeezed his arm and tried to sound calm. "You'll be all right!"

But Kate wasn't sure that her brother would be all right. So much blood! She could even see part of a white leg bone, but couldn't tell if all of his leg was there.

Bits of blood and clothing scattered nearby suggested what had happened. The ditch was partially hidden by the tall brush, so maybe J.T. hadn't seen it. The tractor could have been thrown off balance and started to topple over, enough to make J.T. fall. Kate cringed at the thought of those powerful Bush Hog blades tearing into her brother's leg.

J.T. moaned. "Kate, help me."

Kate whipped her sweatshirt off and gently wrapped it around her brother's blood-soaked leg. Her hands were shaking, but she spread her fingers as wide as she could and squeezed, hoping to stop the bleeding. Still, the blood came. She needed help. Reaching with one hand for her cell phone, she felt only a flat pocket. She'd left the phone back on her desk. Her heart dropped. She was on her own then. What was she going to do to stop the blood? Make a tourniquet?

How do you make a tourniquet? Desperately, she tried to recall what she'd learned from a first aid session years ago. A group of homeschoolers had met at the fire department one evening. They took turns bandaging one another's arms. Someone had showed them how to stop bleeding with a belt—that was a last resort. The tightened belt cut off the blood supply. But it also meant a person would probably lose that limb, Kate recalled. No way was she going to do that. Still, Kate took note that J.T. had worn a belt that day.

Pressure points, she suddenly remembered. There were pressure points to stop bleeding, but where exactly were they?

All she could do was squeeze hard. She stretched her hands as much as she could trying to wrap her fingers around J.T.'s lower thigh. Up on her knees, leaning into her arms, she pressed down with everything she had.

Dazed, J.T. tried to sit up.

"No—lie down," Kate told him. "It's okay. You're going to be okay."

While her brother fell back, Kate kept up the pressure. But was she pressing hard enough to stop the bleeding? There was so much blood it was hard to tell.

The tractor's noise grew louder. Unbelievably, it was circling back toward them—like an enemy! She would have to move her brother or else stop the tractor. It wasn't going fast, probably just second gear. If she grabbed onto the back, and climbed up to where they'd stood as kids getting rides, maybe she could pull herself up onto the seat and slam it out of gear.

She kept squeezing.

It wouldn't work, though, standing on the back of the tractor, she realized. The PTO was there, the equipment that connected the tractor to the Bush Hog.

Panicked, Kate turned back to J.T. "The tractor's coming back! What should I do?"

Her brother didn't answer.

"J.T.! The tractor's coming back! How do I stop it?!"

"Run alongside," J.T. said weakly. "Reach in . . . hit the gear-shift." He grimaced before finishing. "Put it in neutral."

Kate must have looked terrified.

"You can do it," J.T. told her. "Don't be afraid, Kate."

He was telling *her* not to be afraid?

"Okay, but when I let go, J.T., you have to keep squeezing your leg. You've got to stop the bleeding."

Kate helped her brother roll over on his side so it was easier for him to keep his hands on the injured leg. "Get a good grip. That's it. Now squeeze as hard as you can!"

Standing up, Kate fixed her bearings and took off running through the brush toward the tractor. Sharp prickers tore at her legs, and the tall grass made it hard to see where she was running, but she raced on, falling once over an unseen rock. Up and running again, she plunged forward until she was along-side one of the tractor's large back wheels. She could see the gearshift with the bulbous end, but there was no way for her to reach in and hit it. She couldn't get close enough.

She kept running, trying to figure out what to do next, then suddenly, the tractor hit the same drainage ditch it must have hit before and toppled. The Bush Hog flipped over too, its sharp blades still spinning. Quickly, Kate scrambled over the tractor's wheel and reached in to turn the key that shut off the engine.

In the eerie quiet that followed, she rushed back to J.T. Care-fully, she removed his hand on the saturated sweatshirt and replaced it with her own, but she couldn't tell if the bleeding had stopped or not.

J.T. curled his mouth in pain.

Should she run for help? Should she stay and try to stop the bleeding? Tears sprang into Kate's eyes. Why hadn't she slipped her cell phone into her pocket like she always did?

Blood was pooling on the ground.

Kate swallowed hard. She had to make a decision.

"Help me," J.T. begged.

Sucking in her breath, Kate reached for her brother's belt. Quickly, she pulled it from his waist, then slipped it around the mid part of his thigh, above his knee, and pulled it through the buckle again. She paused before pulling it tight. She wasn't a doctor—she wasn't *sure*! But bottom line, she didn't want her brother to bleed to death on the ground beside her.

Up on her knees, Kate used all her strength to pull the belt tight with one hand and push down on J.T.'s leg with the other.

Her brother grimaced.

Kate pulled even tighter.

"Can you reach down and hold it?" she asked J.T.

"I can try," he mouthed, opening his hand.

Kate helped to wrap the end of the belt twice around his fingers so it wouldn't loosen up.

"I'm going for help," Kate said. "Can you hold on, J.T.?"

His eyes were closed, but he moved his head to indicate "yes."

Kate burst into the house just as her mother was coming down the front stairs.

"Mom, call for help! J.T. fell off the tractor!"

"Where is he?" Her mother flew down the stairs.

Breathless, Kate grabbed the bottom of the banister. "The field!"

Her mother gasped upon seeing the blood on her hands.

"Up toward Beck's old place!" Kate told her. "The overgrown field!"

Kate's mother rushed to the phone in the living room.

"Tell them the Bush Hog cut his leg! A lot of bleeding!"

Kate dashed to the bathroom, grabbed all the clean towels she could find and was running back through the house when her mother hung up the phone and stopped her.

"I'll go!" her mother exclaimed, reaching for the towels and thrusting the phone toward Kate. "Stay and direct the ambulance!"

Kate ran with her mother partway through the first soybean field until they could both see the toppled tractor. "He's just beyond it," Kate told her.

When her mother ran ahead, Kate returned to the front yard and anxiously awaited the ambulance. It came just a few minutes later, its lights flashing, followed by a fire truck. Kate pointed to the fields. "He's out there!"

"Run ahead and show us," someone called out the window. "We'll have to go slow over the crops."

Kate took off and the vehicles followed. But they could only go so far. The paramedics finally had to get out and follow Kate on foot, jogging with their equipment.

When they arrived at the scene, J.T. was lying with his head in his mother's lap. Kate was able to see that it was Brady's cousin Carl who had responded with the ambulance. "Let's get that leg elevated," Carl said. After he and Kate's mother carefully repositioned J.T., Carl ripped open a bandage pack.

Suddenly, there was Brady! He must have been riding along

with his older cousin. She watched, astonished, as Brady kneeled beside J.T.

A woman medic started an IV while Carl unwound the bloody towels and pressed thick wads of clean gauze against the wound. Kate spied J.T.'s broken glasses in the grass nearby. She picked them up and stood watching, her eyes brimming with tears, and a tight, sticky fist at her mouth.

While Carl and Kate's mother worked together to press the gauze pads on the largest leg wound, it was Brady who stayed by J.T.'s shoulders and took one of his bloodied hands in his own. Brady's familiar voice was strong and calm. "Hey, J.T., can you hear me? It's gonna be all right, man," he told his old friend. "We got here as quickly as we could. You're gonna be all right now."

~21~
WHEN EVERYTHING CHANGED

Kate stood at a window in the high-rise hospital's waiting room and stared into a dense gray fog that covered the city streets. A yellow traffic light blinked through the heavy mist, and portions of other buildings poked through. But there was one thing Kate saw clearly: how all of life's priorities had suddenly lined up differently. Bullies, cheaters, chickens being fed arsenic and antibiotics—they weren't even in the picture anymore. Homecoming dances, field hockey games, good grades—who cared? The one and only thing that mattered was that her brother lived.

She didn't even care if J.T. lost his leg. She knew that lots of people lived full lives with artificial limbs. She'd seen how brave soldiers who lost legs in war went on to play basketball, climb mountains, and run races.

The tractor. In her mind, she saw it lying on its side in the field, the evil Bush Hog behind it. Would they even want to keep it? How would they get it back in the shed? Uncle Ray, probably. Uncle Ray would know how to right the tractor. And of course they wouldn't get rid of it. Too wasteful. But Kate would always hate the sight of it.

They had left the farm in such a hurry. Kate's mother went with J.T. in the ambulance while Kate had to wait for Aunt Helen to come pick up Kerry. Then out of the blue, Jess's mother was there offering to drive Kate all the way to the hospital in Baltimore. It fell to Aunt Helen to make an evening check on the chickens because Uncle Ray was in bed, recovering from shoulder surgery. In North Carolina, Kate's grandmother had already started the long trip back to Maryland. Everyone was scrambling to help. Kate was grateful for the circle of friends and family they had.

Despite the early hour, just past dawn, the waiting room was more than half full; there were more than a dozen people, some flipping through magazines, some stretched out trying to sleep on chairs using sweaters and jackets for blankets. Still others sipped drinks out of Styrofoam cups and watched a muted television that was streaming the news and commercials about yogurt and new cars, a reminder of how tragedies coexisted with day-to-day life. Nothing ever stopped, Kate realized over the long night. Even on the happiest of days in the future—if those days ever came again—this space would be full of people waiting, scared and on edge, like her, for news that could change their lives forever.

"I came as quickly as I could!" Miss Hatcher exclaimed, bursting into the waiting room. J.T.'s probation officer opened her arms to Kate.

Kate was astonished to see her. She hadn't thought a probation officer would care so much. But all along Miss Hatcher had said she liked J.T. and wanted to see him "back on track." Her driving all the way to Baltimore in the predawn darkness was proof that it was more than just a job to her.

"How's he doing?" she asked, giving Kate a hug.

"Mom is talking to the doctors right now. He lost a lot of blood," Kate said, feeling her voice grow shaky. "One leg was cut up really bad."

The two of them sat down together in seats near the window. Miss Hatcher took one of Kate's hands while Kate tried to tell her what had happened.

Not too long afterward, Kate's mother came into the room. Her eyes were moist and red, and her hair bedraggled and messy. Kate and Miss Hatcher rushed to meet her.

"He's going to be okay," Kate's mother said with a tired smile, her eyebrows lifting slightly.

"What about his leg?" Kate asked.

Her mother's smile brightened. "He didn't lose it."

And just like that, everything changed. Relief and happiness. A huge weight was suddenly gone. Her brother would live—and he would live with both his legs.

"Thank you, Kate," her mother murmured, enfolding Kate in her thin arms. "You saved his life. They say if you hadn't stopped that bleeding, he surely would have bled to death."

Kate pulled back. "But what about the belt? The tourniquet? It didn't cut the blood off?"

"It helped stop the bleeding but wasn't tight enough to cut all the blood off."

"So, because I didn't do such a great job with the tourniquet, he has his leg?"

Kate's mother hugged her again.

Amazing. Kate squeezed her eyes shut and enjoyed the odd but happy feeling of knowing that she had messed up so badly.

Since J.T. was deep asleep and couldn't be disturbed, they decided that it would be best if Miss Hatcher took Kate home while Kate's mother stayed at the hospital for another day or two. There was a house nearby where parents of hospitalized children could stay for free.

"You'll need to do all the chores for your brother," her mother said. She looked Kate in the eye and put a hand on her shoulder. "Do you understand what that means?"

She didn't have to spell it out. Kate knew that "all the chores" included the culling. She'd have to select the damaged or different chicks and get rid of them.

"Kate?"

She didn't hesitate a second time. "It's fine."

"The company will be out tomorrow afternoon to check," her mother said. "You'll have to be ready for them."

"I'll have it done," she promised. "Don't worry."

The long ride home went surprisingly fast. Miss Hatcher stopped at a drive-through restaurant to buy them burgers and drinks, but Kate wasn't hungry. She held an icy soda in her hands, but didn't have much appetite and set the bag of food on the floor by her feet. At first, they didn't talk. Kate stared out the window, watching buildings, houses, and shopping centers blur together as they passed by.

"Just when things were going so well for J.T.," Kate said after a while.

"I know. *Now*, of all times," Miss Hatcher agreed. "Although there's never a good time for an accident. You know that, right?"

"That's true," Kate agreed.

"I've gotten to know your brother a little," Miss Hatcher went on. "He is not going to let this get him down. He's come through too much already. The kayak incident, the juvenile detention center, your father's death, that bully from the eighth grade—"

"What? Did J.T. tell you about him?" Kate asked.

Miss Hatcher leaned forward to settle her coffee in the dashboard holder and kept driving. "Yeah. One day he told me about this kid. I forget, what's his name?"

"Curtis," Kate said.

"Curtis, right. And there was another one."

"Hooper?" Kate asked.

"Maybe. Although I'm not sure he ever told me the other one's name. Anyway, J.T. told me how Curtis really made his life miserable back in the eighth grade by calling him Chicken Man and being pretty nasty. But then he said while Curtis started up again in high school, he had suddenly backed off. He said Curtis even nodded at him one day in school, almost like he was saying, "Sorry, man.""

Kate was surprised. Why hadn't J.T. ever mentioned that?

"Here's the thing that impressed me about the bully thing," Miss Hatcher continued. "J.T. said he actually understood why Curtis first bullied him."

Kate turned to her. "What did he say?"

"Let me think. He said it was because he thought Curtis was angry at the world. He'd lost his older brother, someone he cared about a lot. And apparently, he had just moved to this area and didn't have many good friends, just this one kid at school who was kind of a loner."

"Definitely Hooper," Kate said.

Miss Hatcher glanced over at Kate. "Maybe. Like I said, I don't think he mentioned a name. Whoever it was, the bully just hung out with that one kid."

"It's kind of sad," Kate said. "Because that other boy, Hooper, and my brother have a lot in common. They're both smart. They're both computer geeks. I don't know why Hooper wouldn't like J.T., or why he'd want to pick on him."

"Does Hooper have friends other than Curtis?" Miss Hatcher asked.

Kate shook her head slowly. "I'm not sure, but I don't think so."

Miss Hatcher drove for a while and then said, "Well, you know what I think? I think this kid, Hooper, has even bigger problems than Curtis."

And all of a sudden, a possibility occurred to Kate. Had she been cheating for Hooper, and not Curtis?

Maybe not that first assignment for Creative Writing, but then something must have happened, because a chunk of time went by before she had to write all those papers for ancient history and English. Maybe that was why Curtis had *Huckleberry Finn*. He wasn't reading *Animal Farm*, Hooper was! Was Hooper forcing Curtis to make Kate cheat? Was the bully being bullied?

It would also explain why Curtis said he couldn't stop the cheating. And why he said it was out of his hands.

But if so, *why*? What power did Hooper have over Curtis?

Kate rubbed her forehead. Maybe she was wrong.

"Goodness, you're thinking awfully hard about something," Miss Hatcher observed as she reached for her coffee again.

Kate faced forward again and crossed her arms. "I'm just putting some pieces together," she said.

When they turned up the driveway to Kate's house, Tucker came bounding down the driveway to meet them.

"Oh, no. We must have left him outside," Kate said, feeling bad they'd forgotten him. "Everything yesterday happened so fast."

Miss Hatcher slowed down so as not to hit the dog and they inched their way around the circular part of the driveway in front of the Tylers' house. After Kate got out of the car, she kneeled to greet Tucker.

"Are you sure you'll be okay on your own?" Miss Hatcher asked through the open door. She leaned over to hand Kate her bag of food.

"I'll be fine," Kate assured her. "Really. I've got the chores to do—and I've got Tucker. He'll protect me."

"What about dinner?"

Kate smiled wanly and held up the bag. "Plus I'm pretty good at cooking," she said. "And anyway, my aunt Helen is coming over with my sister and said she'd bring something to eat."

"Okay, but if you need anything, you give me a holler, you hear?"

"I promise I will," Kate said. "Thank you so much."

Kate closed the car door and kneeled to hold Tucker back while Miss Hatcher drove away. Home alone now, she almost felt numb—and weirdly suspended in time, as though she were outside of her own life looking down on it. There were so many mixed emotions from the past twenty-four hours that she couldn't feel any one of them. Of course she was happy that J.T. was going to be okay. She still couldn't believe Brady had come with the ambulance. And was it possible that Hooper, not Curtis, was the bully in her life? Although, with J.T.'s tragic accident, wouldn't that whole episode be over? Someday she wanted to understand it all. Overwhelmed, she sank down on the bottom step of the porch. When Tucker sat close beside her, Kate put an arm around the dog.

"J.T.'s going to be okay," she whispered into Tucker's fur. "He'll be home soon, okay?"

Something else, though. Something else bothered her. The culling. Slowly, Kate straightened up. The chicks were two weeks old now. It would be obvious that some were not growing at the same rate as the others. She needed to separate—and get rid of them.

Could she do it?

She'd promised her mother she would. The chicken people would be out tomorrow to check. She would be staying home from school in order to let them in.

Kate swallowed hard and felt a slight wave of nausea as she turned to gaze across the yard at the two chicken houses. Giant fans that once sucked in fresh air at the ends of the buildings were still, all the windows sealed shut. There were thousands of chickens inside. Probably dozens of them were "different." Crippled. Bent necks. Blind. Sick. Some simply smaller—although maybe they'd catch up with a little time. Kate wondered: Did the company ever think of that?

Tucker nudged her hand, but Kate remained still and for a long time simply stared across the yard.

Then she dropped her eyes and went inside to prepare herself.

~22~
PLAYING GOD

Of course there was a procedure for it. For the killing. It was called "cervical dislocation." It meant breaking the chick's neck. Death was supposedly instantaneous.

A few years ago, when Kate was nine and J.T. was ten, the two of them had been taught how to do it. Kate remembered exactly where they stood in one of the chicken houses, just inside the door beside the gray, metal fuse box on the wall. She remembered peering down at the few day-old chicks her father had selected. They waited in a white, plastic bucket, their little feet tapping the bottom. Kate diverted her eyes to stare at the cement floor beneath her feet, because it suddenly dawned on her what was actually going to happen.

Her father had not asked Kate to watch. He had asked J.T. But she'd been curious, and she hadn't wanted to be left out.

"Why can't I go?" she'd pressed her father at the kitchen door.

"I don't think you'd like it, Katie Bug. Maybe when you're older."

"But J.T. is only a year older than me."

Her father had sighed. Big sigh, if she remembered right.

"You said it was part of the business," Kate had argued. "I want to help, too."

So Kate's father had shrugged, and they'd walked across the yard together.

Kate's father was not a mean person. He was a kind man with a big heart who stopped his tractor to move turtles in the fields. When he picked up one of the chicks with his large, callused farmer's hands, he did it gently. He supported the small bird in his palm with two fingers, so Kate and J.T. could see how its head hung forward, toward its chest. "It's called a crookneck," her father explained. "All the chicks are vaccinated before they come to us, but sometimes the needle doesn't go in the right place. It'll never be able to hold its head up. These are some of the chicks we have to cull."

Kate felt sorry for the chick and peered up at her father.

He must have sensed what she was feeling. "They don't know what's coming," he told her, his voice soft, but matter-of-fact. "It's over before they can react."

She wanted to be grown-up and brave like J.T., so she nodded vigorously that she understood and watched, wide-eyed, but still fearful, while her father positioned his fingers behind the chick's neck. With a flick of his thumbs, he quickly separated, internally, the chick's head from its spine. He'd said it would be instant death, but the little chick was still moving its legs afterward, and Kate couldn't watch anymore. She turned away, her eyes filling with tears, and bolted from the building.

"Kate!" her father called.

But Kate didn't stop. She ran back across the yard between the tractor sheds and sprinted between the rows of soybeans all the way down to the river where she sat for a long time, alone, on the fallen locust.

That night, when she and J.T. crawled out onto the roof outside her brother's bedroom window, J.T. confessed how much he hated the culling, too. He said he didn't blame her for running away and gave her a cinnamon-flavored honey stick he'd gotten at Brady's house the day before. He only had the one stick. Funny how she recalled those little details. Maybe it was because after he gave her the honey stick, J.T. promised her, "You won't ever have to do that culling, Kate. I'll do it for you."

Kate had cherished the promise that protected her, even though they never mentioned it again. The promise occupied a special place deep in her heart. Her brother had gone on to say that he'd only watched the culling because he wanted to help. "Dad hasn't been feeling well," J.T. had told her. Looking back, Kate wondered if that was the beginning of her father's illness.

But now that her father was gone and J.T. wasn't there to honor his promise, Kate didn't have a choice. She couldn't run from the chicken house crying. She couldn't leave it to her brother or her uncle Ray. She had to prepare herself.

But *how*?

She pulled out a chair at the kitchen table and sat down. She closed her eyes and tried to imagine what she needed to do— like watching a movie in her head. She would take a big breath and walk into the first house. No crying, because that would make it hard to see the chicks and tell which ones were smaller, or crippled, or different somehow. She would stand as she did the killing, then drop the dead chick in the bucket. *Kill, then drop.* If she moved quickly, she could have it done in an hour.

The phone rang. Kate opened her eyes and undid her fists. She had rolled her fingers in so tightly there were little half-moon marks from her fingernails in the skin of her palms. The phone rang a second time, and Kate got up to answer. It was Aunt Helen saying she'd be right over with Kerry and a casserole she'd made for the girls' dinner. Kate was glad for the distraction and rushed into the kitchen to set places at the table for dinner. She filled two glasses of water and buttered two pieces of bread. She swept the floor and fed Tucker and Jingles and made a note that they needed dog food and milk at the store. She even ran down to the shed with a carrot and some lettuce to feed Hoppy.

Back in the house, she could have gone back to imagining her task, but instead she stood by the front window watching for Aunt Helen's van. When they arrived and Kerry rushed off to find the cat, Kate told Aunt Helen all about the accident and what the doctor said. Aunt Helen gave her a hug and tried to get her to pack some clothes and go home with her, but Kate shook her head. "I have to do J.T.'s chores," she said. "I've got to do the culling before the company people come tomorrow afternoon."

Aunt Helen tried to smile, but she looked worried. "You're a brave girl," she said.

Kate knew better. She was not brave. Not by a long shot.

Her worried face must have prompted her aunt to have a change of heart and not allow the girls to stay alone after all. She set the casserole she'd made into the refrigerator and told the girls to gather their things. "You can do the culling in the morning," she said to Kate. "I'll get you back early."

Kate and Kerry rushed upstairs to pack pajamas and toothbrushes. Kate also grabbed her backpack, and Kerry carried a stuffed lion under her arm.

At Aunt Helen's house, everyone except for Uncle Ray, who was still in bed recovering from his surgery, sat down to eat macaroni and cheese. Kate's three little girl cousins were cute and she adored them, but their questions exhausted her: *When is J.T. coming home? Does he have a nice doctor? What happened to J.T.'s leg? Did it have blood?*

Aunt Helen finally cut them off and opened a tin of cookies that she'd made. Then, when the girls went upstairs to take their baths and go to bed, Kate tucked sheets and a blanket into the living room couch and settled in for the night. Kerry was supposed to sleep upstairs, sharing a bed with her cousin Annie, but soon she was in a sleeping bag, down on the floor beside Kate on the couch, the two of them holding hands, and Aunt Helen let her stay.

Early the next morning, Uncle Ray came downstairs in his bathrobe, his arm in a sling, and sat in the living room armchair while Kate finished folding the sheets she had slept on.

"I know you've got to do the culling this morning," he said. "And I know it's going to be hard for you, Kate. Try not to think about it too much. Pretend you're a robot. That's what I do."

Kate sat with the gathered blanket on her lap and looked at her uncle. It had never occurred to her that the culling had bothered him, too. Uncle Ray reached over and touched her knee. "You need to do it for your family, Kate. You've got to help out for a while, now that J.T.'s down and I'm laid up."

She nodded. "I understand," she said. "Don't worry, Uncle Ray."

"That's the girl."

After Aunt Helen dropped the two girls off at the house, Kate busied herself with chores and continued putting it off as long as she could. She fixed a lunch for Kerry and helped her pick out clothes for school. She combed out and braided Kerry's long hair. She fed the dog and the cat, and walked her little sister down the driveway to wait for the bus.

"It's going to be a nice day," Kate said as she took in a big breath of fresh morning air. She hoped to draw in some strength, too, as she surveyed the blue sky and the bright sun rising in the east beyond wide, harvested cornfields full of feasting geese. "If you want, Kerry, after school we'll carve those pumpkins."

"Yay!" Kerry approved. "And Grandma's coming home with Mommy! They're going to make an apple pie! Grandma said I could help. But we'll do the pumpkins first, okay?"

"You got it," said Kate.

Kerry's agenda for the day was far simpler. Kate envied her innocence.

The bus appeared, its brakes wheezing, and rumbled to a stop in front of them. "Have fun at school!" Kate told her sister. She smiled and blew a kiss when Kerry waved back through the window.

As the bus pulled away, a dark, sinking feeling took hold again. Kate would be missing school again because of the chore that lay ahead. And there was no more putting off what needed to be done.

By two o'clock, it was all over. The culling, the visit from the company inspector, everything. When Kate's mother had called just after one P.M. with the good news that J.T. was awake and doing well and that Grandma had arrived at the hospital, too, Kate was able to offer her own positive report on the farm.

But she was struggling mightily with what she had done.

After hanging up the phone, Kate retreated to her bedroom and picked up her journal. There was an hour before Kerry came home. Maybe writing would help:

I did a terrible job with the culling today. Guess I'm not very good at playing God, deciding who lives and who dies. When I walked into the first chicken house with the flashlight in one hand and the bucket in the other, I was already struggling. There was a dim light over the feeders, so that's where I started. The chicks were only two weeks old, still fuzzy and starting to get white feathers. The first one, which I chose because it was smaller than the others, seemed almost glad to be picked up.

I held that little chick in my hands, then I put my thumbs behind its head. The term "cervical dislocation" stood up in my mind like a billboard. "Instant death," Dad said. "They don't know what's coming." But I remembered what I'd seen.

"I'm so sorry," I told that little chick. Then I squeezed my eyes shut, so I couldn't witness what I had to do.

Only I couldn't do it.

I could not do it.

I hung my head and sat down in the middle of all those chicks with that little one in my hands, and I cried while chicks hopped up on my legs and all over my arms. I didn't care that I was sitting in chicken manure. I let the little chick go, then I put my head in my hands and cried. I thought if I cried hard enough, I could shut the whole thing out.

But I couldn't shut it out. I was stuck.

What happened next is I got scared. Scared of what my mother would say and how she'd react. Scared of what the company people would do when they came. Scared of how disappointed J.T. and Uncle Ray and everyone else would be in me. The fear made me brave. I stood up and collected all the smaller chicks, the ones with broken legs, the ones that looked off, and I put them in the bucket. I had twenty of them in there, climbing over each other and scratching the sides to get out. I thought that if I took them to the outside water spigot I could turn the water on them fast and they'd drown really quick. Somehow, that seemed better than using my bare hands.

I put a few more chicks in the bucket. I had twenty-three. I had to keep count and write the number down. I carried them outside to the water spigot and turned on the water. I lifted the bucket—but I didn't put it under the spigot right away. I held it with the water spurting out, some of it getting my shoes wet and spraying mud all over my legs. The bucket grew heavy. Finally, I turned the water off, because I had an even better idea.

Back inside the chicken house, I had seen this cardboard box. Gently, I dumped the chicks into the box. I gathered more chicks, too, until I had thirty. I folded the top of the box down over them— then I carried the box across the field to the chicken coop next door.

When I let the chicks loose, the three older birds didn't move or even seem interested. Weird, but those chickens never have acted normal. Some of the chicks tried to follow me out the door, but I shooed them back. While I was there, I found my journal and the *pen outside the coop where I'd dropped them yesterday when I ran to help J.T. I put those things in the empty box and returned to cull the other house. So now I have another secret. Plus, I'll have to keep them alive.*

Kate set down her pen and closed up the journal, frustrated that writing didn't bring the closure, or comfort, she was seeking. She pushed the notebook deep inside her backpack and glanced at the clock. It was close to three P.M. She needed to hurry. After pulling her sneakers on, she set off down the driveway to meet Kerry's bus.

~23~
A THEFT

K ate squinted as she peered out the living room window. Was she seeing right? Was that Jess riding a bicycle up the driveway? Jess lived five miles away. They didn't ride bikes back and forth because of the highway. But it was Jess. Did her mother know she'd ridden over?

"Hey! I tried to call you last night!" Jess said, hopping off her bike as Kate walked out to greet her.

"How come you're not at school? At field hockey?" Kate asked.

"Practice got canceled. Coach had to do something."

Jess set the bike down on its side, and the two girls embraced. Jess's face was beaded with sweat, and her cheeks were bright pink.

"You never answered my texts," Jess said.

"Sorry. My phone died," Kate told her. "There was too much going on."

"Gosh, I know. How are you? How's J.T.? All we know is he won't lose the leg."

"He'll be okay," Kate said. "He lost some muscle tissue, and he has about a million stitches, plus some sort of a metal rod and a bunch of plates holding things together. It'll be a long recovery. The doctor said he'd be in a wheelchair for a while, then on crutches, and he'll have to do a lot of physical therapy."

Jess grimaced and put a hand to her mouth. "Poor J.T.," she sympathized. "And *you*, Kate. I mean I can't imagine how awful that was, trying to stop the bleeding. I could *not* have done what you did."

"Yeah, you probably could have," Kate countered gently.

"No way," Jess said.

The two girls walked toward the front porch. "You'd be surprised what you can do when you have to," Kate said. "There's no test for it, you know. There's no way you can find out what you can really do until you're in it."

"That would make a great quote," Jess said. "Finding the strength you didn't know you had."

"You should use it!"

Jess shook her head as the two girls sat down on the porch steps. "I'm not doing the quote thing anymore."

"Why not?"

"Not worth it," Jess said. "Everybody was making fun of me."

"That's a mistake, Jess. Your quotes were good. You shouldn't let Olivia and the others change your mind. You've got to be true to yourself."

"Yeah, well, it's hard to be true to yourself when people are making fun of you."

She'd have to agree, Kate thought, thinking of how hard it was for J.T. to get his life going with all the bullying.

"Nice pumpkins!" Jess said, spotting the two carved pumpkins on the top step behind them. "But what's that?" she asked, pointing to the stepladder set up nearby, each rung holding a reclining doll.

"That's the doll hospital," Kate explained. "It's a high-rise building, like the one J.T.'s in."

"Cute," Jess said. "And just so you know," she said after a while, "some of us are going to ask Coach Dietrich if you can come back on the team."

"No. Don't," Kate said. "I didn't show up for the game before J.T.'s accident even happened, so there's no excuse. I already had an e-mail from the coach telling me I was off the team."

Jess looked disappointed.

"Hey! Did I see you had green wires in your braces?" Kate asked, trying to lift the mood again.

Jess gave her a big, toothy grin. "You like 'em?"

Kate wrinkled her nose. "Actually, it looks like mold. It looks like you have moldy teeth."

Jess slapped her playfully. "Dummy. I have yellow on the bottom, see?" She showed her. "Green and gold for school. For the field hockey tournament!"

Kate's smile faded. It was an instant reminder that Kate was no longer on the team. Emotions were ricocheting back and forth.

"Hey," Jess said gently, "we're still going to North Carolina this summer, right? To that place where we can hold a baby tiger?"

Kate looked at her friend. "Absolutely."

✶

221

Surprisingly, it was almost a comfort to be back in school. News of the accident had gotten around. All of Kate's teachers expressed concern for J.T.—and for Kate, too, wondering if there was anything they could do to help.

"It's really awful about J.T.," Curtis said, waiting for Kate to come out of Creative Writing.

"Thanks," Kate replied.

"Look, I have to explain something to you," he said, leaning in toward her as they walked. "Can you meet me after school by the labs?"

"It needs to be quick," Kate said. "I have to catch the bus, because I'm not staying for field hockey anymore."

"How come?" Curtis asked.

"I missed a game, so I'm off the team."

Curtis kept pace with Kate, but only for a few steps. He didn't say anything more, and Kate didn't turn around, but she had the feeling he was watching her as she walked away.

They met in the usual spot between restrooms on the second floor. Kate hadn't noticed earlier, but Curtis had a haircut, and his hair wasn't down in his eyes the way it usually was.

Because she had all her books for the work she had missed over the past couple days, Kate's backpack was heavy, and she let it drop to the floor. She stood in front of Curtis and crossed her arms.

"Okay," she prompted.

Curtis fidgeted with his hands. "So anyway, you don't have to do that last assignment."

"No. I wasn't going to," Kate said.

Curtis nodded like he'd expected that response. "Is J.T. going to be okay?"

She could have said, *Why would you care?* But she didn't. She took a deep breath. "He has a long road ahead of him, but he'll be all right."

"Good," Curtis said. He was nodding again. It must have been a nervous gesture, Kate thought. "Good," Curtis repeated, "because man, that was pretty awful. When I heard it was a Bush Hog, I didn't think he'd come through in one piece."

"Well, he didn't really," Kate said. "His leg will never be the same, because of the muscle he lost." She uncrossed her arms, but still kept her eyes averted.

"Gosh, I didn't mean to say that. What I meant is he's lucky he's not dead."

Kate nodded, but tears slowly welled up in her eyes after the reminder of what could have happened.

"Look, I know the feeling," Curtis said. "When my brother's tank got hit—over in Afghanistan—I couldn't sleep. I couldn't even eat."

Kate looked up at him. "Is that how he got killed?"

"No. He got injured in the explosion. A bad head wound, but he lived. He came home then. He got a Purple Heart."

"My father has a Purple Heart," Kate said.

"What? Your dad was in the service?" Curtis asked.

"He was in the Gulf War. That's why he's buried at Arlington."

"Oh. Wow. I didn't know your dad was gone."

"A year ago, just after J.T. got sent away," Kate said. She frowned a little. "You didn't know that?"

Curtis shook his head slowly. "No. I didn't. How would I know?"

"Look," Kate said, "I really have to get going—"

"Okay," Curtis replied. He pulled his hands back out of his jeans pockets and opened them, but then he didn't seem to know what to do with them and hooked his thumbs in his two front pockets. "So I said I'd explain. I just want you to know that it wasn't me. All those weeks, making you cheat, it wasn't for me."

Curtis looked over her shoulder to peer down the hallway. "Kate, can we just step around the corner?"

Kate looked down the hallway, too, but there were just a couple kids, walking in the opposite direction. "What are you afraid of?"

"I'm not afraid of anything. I just don't want to be seen."

"By *who*?"

Curtis didn't answer.

"Are you afraid Hooper is going to see you here?"

Curtis hesitated, but then he nodded. "Yeah."

"I was cheating for Hooper, wasn't I?"

"What? You knew?"

"I figured it out," Kate said.

"He's got something on me. I'm sorry, Kate. I should never have let this happen."

"No. You shouldn't have! I totally agree!"

"I am so sorry."

"You *should* be sorry!"

Curtis dropped his head, and despite all the anger that she had felt in the past, Kate felt flat. Maybe because all the anger that had been building up had been blown away by J.T.'s accident. That, or else maybe she was tired of being angry. At least the bullying was over and she had her apology.

"So what does Hooper have on you?" Kate asked.

"He knows stuff."

"He knows stuff," Kate repeated. "Like what?"

"He knows stuff about my brother. Like if I didn't make you write those papers he was gonna make a Facebook page and put it out there."

Kate narrowed her eyes at Curtis. "Put *what* out there?"

"Information about my brother!"

"Your brother in the army?"

Curtis pressed his lips together and looked uncomfortable.

"Yeah," he finally said. "Hooper was gonna tell the world that my brother didn't die a hero like everybody in this town thought. You know, they wrote that article about him in the local paper, and there was a scholarship in his name at his high school, from people who donated money."

Kate recalled only that Curtis's brother had visited her fifth-grade classroom. She had never known about the newspaper story or the scholarship. Things happened to other people, and sometimes you just didn't know.

"He didn't die a hero," Curtis went on, "because he killed himself."

Curtis wiped at his eyes, and Kate could see how much this hurt him to talk about. She wondered what Justin had done to kill himself—and *why*. She had every reason in the world not to care a whit about Curtis, who had been so mean to her and J.T., but she couldn't help feeling a little sorry for him, too.

"Look, I think maybe you've built something up in your head," Kate suggested. "I don't mean to make it sound like it wasn't huge, but honestly, Curtis, I don't think most people around here would make a big deal out of that."

Curtis frowned. Like maybe that hadn't even occurred to him.

"I mean, your brother didn't grow up here or go to Corsica High."

Suddenly, there was the sound of running footsteps.

Curtis and Kate both stepped around the corner and saw Hooper smack open the double doors at the far end of the hall and disappear with Kate's backpack.

"Stop!" Curtis yelled.

"Oh, great!" Kate said, holding up her hands. "Now, why did he do that?"

"Just to be a pain in the butt," Curtis said. His eyes flashed, and there was a hard, determined set to his jaw. "Don't worry— go catch your bus. I'll get it back."

When Curtis stomped off after Hooper, Kate glanced at her watch. If she didn't run, she wouldn't make it to the bus on time.

Nervous, Kate chewed on her bottom lip the entire ride home. All her books and assignments were in the backpack. How was she going to get her homework done? Should she call school when she got home and report the theft? If she did, would she mention Hooper's name? And then would it all come out about the cheating? Did she want that to happen?

Kate decided it was best to just chill for a while and hope Curtis could get it back. At least she had her cell phone in her denim skirt pocket and her purse was safely on her shoulder.

When she got off the bus, Kate saw that a big combine had

started harvesting the soybeans and was stirring up a huge cloud of dust. She hurried up the driveway. Inside the house, she listened to a voice mail from her mother letting her know that she and Kate's grandmother would be home from the hospital around seven. Her mother asked her to take out a meat loaf from the freezer, do the evening check on the chickens, and be sure Kerry changed her clothes after school and did her homework.

An hour, then. Kate had one hour before Kerry got home. Quickly, she took out the meat loaf, then changed into jeans and went down to the chicken houses to scrape a small amount of feed from the feeders and put it in a plastic bag. She avoided the field being harvested and walked over to Beck's on the road.

When she got to the coop next door, some of the little chicks ran to greet her, but the two with broken legs had died. She was relieved, because she knew they had to have been suffering. After dumping the chicken feed into two pie tins, she put the two dead chicks in the plastic grocery bag to take back with her.

She returned home the same way she went, by walking along the road, and was surprised to see a green truck waiting in her yard. Was it Curtis? Quickly, Kate stashed the dead chicks under a bush. She was glad no one else was home.

Curtis came to meet her as she walked up the driveway. Unbelievably, he had her backpack in his hand.

"Oh, my gosh. Thank you so much for getting it back!" Kate exclaimed.

"It wasn't too hard," Curtis said. "Although I had to chase that joker's bus all the way to the other end of the county. When he got off, he just handed it to me with this stupid little grin on his face."

"Well, I appreciate that you got it back so fast. I hope that now we can finally be done with all this."

"Me too. Like I said, I am truly sorry, Kate." He nodded toward the backpack in her arms. "You want to see if everything's in there?"

"I'm sure it is," Kate said, feeling the weight of the pack. "But I'll check." She set the pack on the ground and kneeled to unzip it and root around inside. "All my books are here: math, biology, English, my Chinese workbook . . ."

She paused. A bad feeling was seeping into her veins. She kept looking. Where was her journal? She had written in it yesterday and stuffed it in her backpack. Yes. But that was her personal journal, she suddenly realized, not her school one. She had written about the culling and that she couldn't do it, and she remembered how, frustrated, she had shoved the notebook into her backpack afterward.

Afraid of what she may have done, Kate shot a worried look at Curtis. "I need to run up to my room to check something," she said. "Can you wait a minute?"

"Sure."

Kate rushed inside and up to her room where she spied a notebook on her desk. It was her school writing journal, not her personal one. For sure then, she had put her personal journal into her backpack! The journal in which she had confessed to hiding the chicks next door! The same one in which she'd written about J.T.'s project testing chicken manure!

Kate covered her eyes with disbelief and sank down on the

edge of her bed. Why had she ever written those journals in the same kind of notebook? Stupid! If Hooper had his hands on that journal, he could put her family out of business with one phone call to the chicken company!

She rushed back to Curtis.

"He's got my journal!" she exclaimed. "He's got my *personal journal*!"

"Hey, calm down, Kate!"

"You've got to get it back, Curtis! *Please!*"

"Why is it so important?"

Kate had to close her eyes to think. Did she really want to tell Curtis? What she had written was not meant for anyone else's eyes—not ever!

"Look, I'll drive over there again and demand that he give it back. I'll punch him out if he doesn't. But really, Kate, what could Hooper possibly do with it?"

What could he possibly do with it? Kate put a hand to her forehead imagining what he could do with it. Curtis—of all people—ought to know what Hooper could do with her personal information.

Curtis jangled the truck keys in one hand and chuckled. "Don't worry, Kate. I'll get him to hand it over."

He still didn't get it. Curtis didn't know how serious this was. If she didn't tell him what she'd written, he wouldn't appreciate how important it was to get the journal back.

Kate brought her hand down and her shoulders slumped. "I guess it's my turn to tell *you* something."

~24~
DIFFERENT

A long, wide piece of white construction paper covered the kitchen table. Kneeling on a chair, Kerry bent over the paper and drew in flowers, stars, and cats with a box of colored markers.

"What else should it say besides 'Welcome Home, J.T.?'" she asked. "And what else should I draw?"

Kate's grandmother set her hands on her hips and surveyed the colorful banner. "J.T. loves being outside. How about some trees and cornfields? And Tucker! You need to draw a dog!"

"You're right, Grandma! I forgot!"

Kate's mother, who was drying the dishes from dinner, smiled.

It would be wonderful to have J.T. home again—and so soon, Kate thought. He'd only been in the hospital a week. Kate had returned once to see him. But she'd heard that Brady Parks had been there twice.

Everyone was glad J.T. was recovering so quickly, and plans

were being made for his homecoming meal: his favorite spaghetti, with coconut cake for dessert this time. To make the occasion even more special, both Jess and J.T.'s friend Ashley had been invited as well. Despite the excitement, Kate's mind and emotions were a mixed bag. Four days had passed since her journal had been taken, and there was still no word from Hooper.

At school the next day, a Friday, Kate and Jess walked downstairs from their last-period math class together.

"Looking forward to the dinner tonight," Jess said. "You sure there's nothing I can bring? J.T. loves brownies. I could make him some."

"That would be really sweet," Kate said. "Remember, no nuts."

"Right! But extra chocolate chips!"

At the bottom of the stairway, the girls split up. Jess went on to field hockey while Kate pretended to rush off to catch her bus. *Pretended* because she skirted the front doors, then walked past the school office and down the hall that led to an exit near the student parking lot.

Outside, she scanned the vehicles for Curtis's green pickup. Dark clouds scudded across the sky, and it was beginning to sprinkle. *Where is he?* she fretted. She didn't want anyone seeing her climb into his truck.

When she spotted him backing out of a parking space, Kate stepped to the side and faked a cough. Curtis pulled up beside her and popped open the passenger door. Kate hopped inside.

"I cleaned up for you," Curtis said. "Hauled out a whole bag of trash from this junk heap!"

Kate was not in the same jovial mood. This wasn't a date! She still felt weird about accepting a ride home with Curtis. She was only doing it because he'd offered to stop at the hardware store so she could buy a bag of chicken feed and get it delivered to the Beck property for her chicks.

Heavy splats of rain started hitting the windshield. Kate was glad. It would be more difficult for anyone to see her through the windows.

"Have you heard from Hooper yet?" she asked. "Was he in school today?"

Curtis shook his head. "No. He lives with his dad, but he spends weekends with his mom, and sometimes he goes early. I bet that's where he's at."

"But he's been gone almost all week."

"I know."

"Where does his mom live?" Kate asked.

"Somewhere down toward Salisbury, I think."

Kate sighed. Salisbury was nearly an hour away.

"Did you try calling him?"

"Yeah. He won't answer."

They rode in silence for a moment as Kate struggled with her mounting anxiety.

"First stop, Perkins Hardware, right?" Curtis asked.

"Yes," Kate said. "I really appreciate it."

"After you told me about J.T.'s project and how they might be putting all that bad stuff in chicken feed, I was thinkin' I might stay away from those chicken nuggets for a while. Hey! If you're gonna raise a flock of chickens, they may as well be healthy."

Kate turned to him. "You know, that's what I thought, too. I could have kept on taking feed from the chicken house, but part of me was curious to see how they'd turn out if they ate feed that didn't come from the company."

"It's too bad you couldn't get some fresh eggs out of those chickens."

"Huh. I never thought of that," Kate said. "But why not? Although I'd have a hard time explaining it to my mother."

"Don't you need a rooster to get eggs?"

Kate smiled sheepishly. "You're kidding me, right?"

Curtis threw her a confused look.

"Oh, my gosh, you don't know!" She stifled a grin. "Sorry. I shouldn't laugh because a lot of people don't understand. But hens lay eggs all the time—with or without a rooster around. That's how we get the eggs we eat! You do need a rooster to fertilize the eggs and get more chicks."

"Ah, okay. I get it," Curtis said. He thumped the steering wheel. "Cool!"

Curtis chuckled, but not Kate. Talk of roosters was only a reminder that in factory farming for chicken meat and eggs the male chicks were killed soon after they were hatched because only females were useful. She remembered her father once saying that a baby rooster was "an unwanted byproduct." Kate never asked him how they were killed. There were some things in the family business she didn't really want to know.

"But one day," Curtis said, wagging his finger, "you *could* get a rooster if you wanted a bigger flock, right?"

Kate rolled her eyes and allowed herself to lighten up. "Boy, we'd really be in trouble then. In the eyes of Valley Shore Chicken Farms, I'm already a thief. If they find out their chickens were turned into laying hens, they'd go ballistic."

"Well, your secret is safe with me," Curtis assured her.

Something about that statement wiped away any of the humor they had just shared. What in the world was she doing *laughing with Curtis Jenkins*?

At the hardware store, Kate and Curtis both went in so Curtis could carry the heavy bag of feed out to the truck. From there it was only a ten-minute drive to the Beck place. Curtis drove slowly, splashing through puddles along the bumpy, overgrown driveway. Once he had to stop to move a branch out of the way. When they were behind the abandoned farmhouse, Curtis parked and carried the bag of feed until it got so heavy he couldn't. Together, they pulled the bag through the tall grass the rest of the way.

Kate held the door open for Curtis and then closed it against the rain. "These are my refugees. Fifty-five of them now," Kate said, shaking the water from her hands as the chicks eagerly gathered around her feet. She pointed to the three older birds. "I don't know about them. They don't do anything but sit there."

"Hmmmm. Antisocial," Curtis observed.

Kate picked up a jug of water and poured some into two pie tins. "Can I ask you something, Curtis?"

He shrugged. "Sure."

Kate stood with the jug in her hands. "Why did you ever become friends with Hooper Delaney in the first place? I mean, he's kind of sketchy, isn't he?"

"People thought I was kind of sketchy, too," Curtis responded. "When I first moved here and was new, no one was nice to me. But I know it's because I had a chip on my shoulder.

I was mad at my mom for leaving my father, and Justin had just gone off to the army. Hooper, he was a loner, too, so we just kind of hung out together. I played a lot of computer games with him, and he came over a few times. He didn't seem to care if I had a crazy family."

"What do you mean, *crazy*?" Kate asked. She screwed the top back on the jug and set it down.

"You know, when my brother first came home, he did a lot of weird stuff. Like this one time my mom closed the kitchen cabinet too loud, and Justin threw himself on the floor thinking it was a bomb going off. He broke his front tooth! Hoop was there that day, and he didn't freak out or anything. Maybe because he didn't have much of a family himself. No brothers or sisters. He always said he'd rather live with his mother, and I know it's because his father's real strict."

"He kind of scares me," Kate said. "Do you think he's the kind of kid who would, like, go off the deep end and do something violent?"

Curtis thought about it for a few seconds, then shook his head. "I don't think so—but who knows? He's got some personal problems going on, for sure. He has trouble talking to people and writing, which is why he hit you up for help on those reports. Math is a breeze for him.

"Aside from that, I think he's just lonely," Curtis said. "He's got an aquarium with fish, and every one of those fish has a name. He's got this one goldfish named Starlight that's, like, ten years old. I told Hoop one day that he ought to go down to the pound and get a dog or something."

Kate dumped the rest of an old bag of feed into two other pie tins for the chicks.

While she worked, Curtis kept talking. "It was Hooper's idea, you know, to pick on J.T. in eighth grade. I'm not sayin' that just to lay blame on him 'cause I'm the one who bullied J.T. But Hoop, all along he was pushin' me. I don't know why I went along with it. I didn't think too much about it. Just did it. That chip on my shoulder, I guess."

Kate had kneeled to shake the pie tins and even out the feed, but then she paused. When she stood up again, she asked, "But why J.T.? Why did you guys pick on *him*?"

Curtis kind of shrugged and bounced his shoulders while widening his eyes as if to say *who knows*? But Kate didn't buy it.

"*Why?*" she persisted. "Out of all the kids in school?"

Curtis crossed his arms and tried to think back. "You know what? I think it's because we saw him in the cafeteria one day praying before he ate an ice-cream sandwich. It just hit us both that that was kind of weird."

Kate looked down. "He went through a period when he prayed all the time," she said. "When my dad first got sick. I don't know, I think my brother's faith kept him strong for a long time."

Curtis snorted. "Sorry! I didn't mean no disrespect, Kate. I just don't get it. But then, I never went to church or anything like that. Maybe Hoop and I, we just saw him as kind of *different*, you know? That's all. It wasn't anything more than that. I was angry, Hoop was angry, and J.T. was different. A bad combination, I guess."

Different. Kate sat on an upturned bucket to think about what Curtis had said. How unfair, how *cruel* the boys had been—and for no good reason.

Curtis flipped over another bucket and sat on it. "Now let me ask you something," he said. "Did you ever know somebody who became a complete stranger?"

Kate looked at him. Her mother, she thought immediately, although she didn't say so.

"I never realized how angry I was at the world for what happened to my brother until that night we were texting," Curtis said. "Do you remember? You were asking questions about Justin and then you said we both had a brother we loved a lot. My brother, he was the most important person in my life, but then he went and killed himself, and nobody even knows why."

"Nobody knows?"

"All we know is he came home from the war a changed person. He had that PTSD thing. Do you know what that is?"

Kate nodded. "I think so. Post-Traumatic . . ."

"Stress Disorder," Curtis finished. "You know that Creative Writing profile we have to write? I'm writing about Justin, and this is how it starts. Curtis looked up and closed his eyes. 'In the middle of the night, if I hear the closet door slam in my brother's room, I know it is Justin trying to hide.'"

"Gosh," Kate sympathized.

"Yeah." Curtis opened his eyes. "He had nightmares and woke up sweating and scared that someone was coming to get him."

"Wow," Kate said.

"Thing is, we were getting help. We were close to getting one of those service dogs that would even sleep with him. But then he went and shot himself."

Curtis paused. "You know, I wasn't going to take that essay you wrote for me in Creative Writing. The first one. I knew it was wrong. I knew I'd been doing wrong for a long time, picking on your brother. But then Hoop got on my case, and things snowballed in the other direction. I just didn't think too much about it."

Pretty lame excuse, Kate thought as she stood and slowly crumpled the empty feed bag. She felt bad for Curtis because of his brother, but a stream of images and snatches of sound also ran through her head: a school locker full of feathers, chicken manure in a smashed-down mailbox, a carton of milk exploding on J.T.'s chest, a cruel banner strung up across the school hallway. And a boy's voice yelling, "Chicken Man!" There had been a mountain of pain and humiliation heaped on her brother for a long time.

Kate leveled her eyes at Curtis. "Someday," she told him, "you need to apologize to J.T."

"I know," Curtis readily agreed. "I will. I can promise you that."

~25~
HOMECOMING

Tucker saw them first. Outside on the porch, the dog started barking, and Kerry ran to the front window. "They're here!" she shouted to Kate, who was in the kitchen spreading garlic butter on the French bread while Jess cut cucumbers for the salad.

The girls hurried outside. It had just stopped raining, and the porch steps and sidewalk were slick, forcing them to slow down in their rush to greet J.T. He lay in the backseat of his grandmother's car with pillows propped up behind him. His injured right leg, wrapped heavily in gauze and encased in a splint, stretched across the seat in front of him.

"Welcome home!" Kate exclaimed, leaning in as she opened the car door.

J.T. grinned sleepily. "It's good to be here."

Kate and her mother eased J.T. out of the backseat and got him propped up on crutches. They guided him inside, practically carrying him up the steps, while Kerry and Jess held Tucker back so he wouldn't get in the way.

After they settled J.T. on the living room sofa, Grandma stuffed pillows in here and there, and Kate's mother covered his legs with a blanket. Finally, Tucker was allowed to say hello. With his tail beating back and forth, he nuzzled J.T.'s hand and side and seemed amazingly mindful of the injured leg. After a quick head scratch from J.T., the dog settled down quietly on the floor, tight beside the couch.

"Did you see?" Grandma asked J.T.

Everyone stepped aside so J.T. could view the colorful banner Kerry had taped to the fireplace mantel.

"Beautiful." He winked at Kerry.

A few minutes later, Ashley arrived. When Kate saw how she and J.T. exchanged something special with their eyes, she gave up her seat so Ashley could sit beside her brother. Everyone watched as J.T. opened the gift bag from Ashley and pulled out a computer magazine, an iTunes card, and some candy, his favorite Swedish fish.

A knock at the door prompted Kate's mother to rise. "There were two more people invited," she told them. "I hope you don't mind. Miss Hatcher wasn't able to come, but we do have one other guest." When she opened the door, there stood Brady Parks.

Silence as he stepped into the living room. The air seemed to have gone out of the room. So much had happened between the two boys that Kate hadn't thought she'd ever see Brady in their house again.

"Come on in, Braden!" Grandma urged him, breaking the silence and motioning energetically with her hand. She had always called Brady by his full name. It was nice hearing it, Kate thought, after all the time that had passed.

Brady smiled shyly and timidly approached. He handed J.T. something wrapped in tinfoil. "My mom's banana bread," he said, "no nuts."

J.T. grinned as he took the bread. "Just the way I like it."

"I know," Brady said.

Kate's mother pulled another dining room chair into the circle around J.T. for Brady.

J.T. turned to Ashley. "You know my friend Brady, right?"

Ashley widened her eyes and laughed. "Duh. Of course! We're in the same English class! We were at the hospital together last weekend! Brady's dad gave us a ride up!"

"You were there together?" J.T. touched the palm of his hand to his forehead. "*Whew!* I guess I was pretty much out of it, then!" He rolled his eyes and reached out for Ashley's hand. She blushed, her round, freckled cheeks filling with a rosy color. She had long, straight brown hair with brown eyes to match, a quick smile, and a sweet voice. But most important, she was super nice, Kate thought. Just the kind of girl her brother deserved.

When Ashley took J.T.'s hand with both of hers, it was impossible not to notice. For the briefest moment, Kate's and Brady's eyes connected.

"Okay. Here's what I want to know," Kerry piped up suddenly. "Can you marry a cat?"

Everyone laughed, and Grandma announced it was time to set up the TV trays for dinner so they could eat in the living room surrounding J.T.

"A toast! Welcome home, J.T.!" Grandma announced, raising her glass of ice water. Everyone else lifted glasses of water and

Diet Coke, including J.T., who added, "Thanks, but I also want to toast my sister Kate, who—no slouch—saved my life."

"Hear, hear!" Grandma said.

After eating and taking his pain medication, J.T. immediately cocked his head and fell asleep on the couch. Dessert hadn't even been served, which, Kerry said, meant he was *really, really tired.*

Kate and Jess gathered the dishes, and everyone moved quietly to the kitchen to sit at the table for slices of coconut cake and small chunks of brownies. When they finished, Grandma put the teakettle on while Mom loaded the dishwasher and told the kids to "sit and visit."

"Maybe a homecoming party was too much for J.T.," Jess suggested.

"I don't think so," Kate said. "He seemed really happy. Especially when he saw Ashley." She turned to Brady. "And then *you!*"

"Yeah. No one expected that!" Jess said.

Brady seemed embarrassed. "Yeah. Well. J.T. and I, we're old friends." He paused and rubbed at a spot on his temple, but didn't seem to want to say anything more than that, which was fine, Kate thought.

"I appreciate you all inviting me," Ashley told the group. "I'd really like to help when J.T. comes back to school. I could carry his books and help him get to classes."

"Me too," Brady said eagerly. "I wanted to talk to you guys about that. We could make a schedule and do shifts, helping him get around school."

"Do you and J.T. have any of the same classes?" Jess asked Brady.

"No, but that won't be a problem. I already talked to the assistant principal. He said I could be late to class if I was helping J.T. with his wheelchair or when he's on crutches."

"And I can help him get to Spanish and algebra," Ashley said. "He's actually saving my life in algebra. It's so hard for me."

Kate rolled her eyes. "I dread it next year."

"But you'll have J.T. to help!" Ashley said.

"Hey—and me, too," Brady chimed in. "That's one of my best subjects."

Kate's heart skipped a beat. She would love getting help from Brady!

"J.T. is so incredibly smart," Ashley said. "Last week, before the accident, he was showing me how to do a quadratic equation—just for fun!"

The kids chuckled.

"So do you guys know I had a crush on J.T. in middle school?" Ashley asked.

"No way!" Jess exclaimed.

Ashley confirmed with a nod. "It was middle school, and I thought I was fat and ugly," Ashley told them. "I didn't have much self-confidence. We were in band together, though, and J.T. was always really nice to me."

"It must have been hard to keep it a secret," Jess said.

Ashley wrinkled her nose. "Not really," she disagreed. "I mean, it's not always easy, but you *can* keep a secret if you're careful. I just didn't say anything!"

Kate didn't say it out loud, but she agreed with Ashley. One hundred percent.

~26~
DISCOVERY

Saturday morning, Kate's alarm went off early. Now that the chicks were a little older and more or less uniform, the culling was easier. Still, there would be a few who looked off, and she wanted to quickly relocate them before the rest of her family was up.

After unlocking the back door, she let the dog scamper out first, then softly pulled it closed behind her and held the screen door, too, so it wouldn't clap shut.

A full day of rain had given the world a good rinse. Even the air smelled clean and refreshed. Moisture on the grass sparkled, and the temperature was crisp. The sweatshirt Kate had pulled on felt good.

While Tucker ran off to make his rounds, Kate headed down to the chicken houses to get her chores done. She picked up several dead chicks and buried them in the manure pile beneath the shed. Then she selected a total of eight for culling, put them in the box, and walked across the field.

When she arrived, she discovered a fox, or a dog, had been digging a hole alongside the chicken coop and had almost made it underneath. After settling the chicks inside, she pulled a loose board off a dilapidated coop nearby and used it like a shovel to scoop dirt back into the hole. She put the board over the spot inside the coop where the animal almost got through, then went outside to stomp down the dirt with her feet. After brushing off her hands, she went back in to feed her flock.

The chicks seemed excited to see her and followed her around, which forced Kate to step carefully, almost shuffle, so as not to crush any of the little birds. Whenever she stopped, they pecked at the toes of her sneakers and went nuts for her shoelaces. What did they think? That they were worms? Kate smiled as she ripped open a bag of chicken feed and scooped out some of the grain with an empty coffee can. She sprinkled the feed in the pie tins and was about to scoop up another can full when a noise stopped her.

Straightening up, she held her breath and listened. Suddenly, a loud *click!* Kate stared at the metal latch on the door and watched as it was lifted by the outside handle. She glanced at the board she had just placed inside the coop, but there wasn't time to fetch it.

With a slow and agonizing creak, the door swung inward, and all at once, Kate's mother filled the opening. She had tennis shoes on, but clutched her bathrobe to hold it closed at her neck. Her hair, long and loose, fell over both shoulders. "Oh, my," she said.

Kate's heart fell.

"What is this?" her mother asked.

Where to begin, Kate wondered as she stood motionless, the coffee can of chicken feed still in her hands.

She met her mother's bewildered gaze. "I couldn't do the culling," she confessed.

The chicks were still pecking at her shoes. Tears seeped into her eyes. "I tried, Mom, but I couldn't kill them."

Her mother put a hand on her cheek as she surveyed the small, illicit flock. "I had no idea," she said. "When I looked out the bedroom window and saw you crossing the field with that box . . ."

For a moment neither spoke, but then the corners of her mother's mouth gently lifted, and she opened her arms. "But I *do* understand, Kate."

Kate set the can of feed down, stepped carefully through the chicks, and went to hug her mother.

"I don't blame you," her mother said, wrapping her arms around Kate. "I could never do it, either."

"You're not mad?" Kate asked.

"How could I be angry?"

Kate pulled back. "But it could get us into so much trouble!"

Her mother relaxed her arms, and the two of them stepped back to survey the chicks. "Well, it could certainly get us in trouble," she agreed. "We'll have to think of something."

Surprised—relieved—*overjoyed* at her mother's reaction, Kate finished the feeding while her mother waited.

"A dust bath!" Kate's mother exclaimed, watching as one of the small chickens made a great show of rooting in the floor dirt and debris while ruffling its feathers. "A natural thing for a chicken, but the ones we raise don't even have room to walk around, let alone take a dust bath."

"I know," Kate sympathized. "Even if they have a short life, it would be nice if that life could be normal, wouldn't it?" She finished refreshing the chicks' water.

"Do you know why your father never let me near the chickens?" her mother asked.

Kate set the water jug down. "Actually, I think I do know," she said. "Was it when the company told you to close in the chicken houses?"

"Yes," Kate's mother replied, her gaze growing distant as she remembered. "When the company told us to nail shut all the windows and cover them with blackout curtains so there was no light and no fresh air. That's when I started to lose it. It only made sense to the company—dollar sense, that is. When chickens are in the dark, they think it's night and they don't move around, so they grow faster. It was better for 'feed conversion,' the company said."

She looked up at Kate. "I once asked your father how much time it saved, keeping the birds in the dark that way. Do you know what he said?"

Kate shook her head.

"He told me it shaved off about two days, which meant the company didn't have to pay to keep them alive for that much longer—two days' worth of feed is what it came down to. We couldn't argue. We had to do what the company told us. They owned the chickens, remember? We were being paid to raise them, and our pay was based on pounds of meat.

"With the windows closed, it became our responsibility to keep the chickens cool with fans. We had to dig a deeper well for more water for the cooling pads and buy a new generator in case the electricity went off, because if the birds overheated, thousands of them would die.

"It got harder and harder for me to deal with it. 'It's only business,' your father tried to tell me. But I know it bothered him, too. You know what it's like inside those houses, Kate. It's not humane. The chickens are packed in so tight you can't even see the floor. All they do is eat. Some of them—their internal organs grow so fast—they have heart attacks and keel over dead."

"I know," Kate said. "They flip!"

Kate's mother moved her head back and forth. "I couldn't stand it." She brought her hand down. "One day, I was alone. It was a beautiful day. A day like today! I went down to the chicken houses, and do you know what I did, Kate? I pulled the nails out from two of the window frames. I pushed open the windows, the way we used to, to let in fresh air and light. I was starting on another window when your father came and stopped me. He was so angry. *So angry*. He told me not to ever go near the chickens again."

Kate didn't tell her mother she knew all this because she had witnessed everything that day. What good would it do now? But she would never forget. A little girl's voice, her own, still echoed in her memory: "Mommy, what are you doing?" Her mother hadn't heard her, hadn't seen her either, and Kate was afraid, so she hid behind the tractor, crouching low and watching when her enraged father stormed down the hill. Later, Kate had told J.T., but no one else. They both knew that if there was a beginning to their mother's depression, that must have been part of it. Not long afterward, her mother couldn't handle their home-schooling, and J.T. and Kate were enrolled at public school.

Kate and her mother walked back through the field quietly. There wasn't much more to say. Both of them were troubled by the business that had become their livelihood. At the house, her mother squeezed Kate's shoulders one more time.

"It's not so bad, is it?" Kate asked. "Keeping the chicks at Beck's place? No one goes there."

"But it won't always be the case," her mother said. "Who knows when they'll try to sell the property? We'll talk about it later. Meantime, we need to get on with the day."

Kate returned to her room and saw on her cell phone that she'd received a text message.

Curtis: U there? I heard from Hooper.

Kate sat on her desk chair texting back.

Kate: What did he say?

Curtis: Gotta be quick. Am at work. Hooper said if u didn't do the report on highroglyphics (sp??) by Monday he would do a Facebook page on Justin, then squeal about the chickens and JT's project.

Kate's shoulders drooped.

Kate: What did you tell him?

Curtis: That I needed to talk to u.

Pause.

Curtis: So what do I say?

Kate: Tell him to meet us by the labs upstairs.

Curtis: U sure?

Kate: Yes.

Curtis: *U going to write that report?*

Kate: *No.*

Curtis: *But tell him to meet us?*

Kate: *Yes.*

Curtis: *I don't get it.*

Kate: *Just tell him to meet us. I have a plan.*

~27~
WHO'S THE BULLY NOW?

Kate had expected Hooper Delaney to be one of the homeliest people in the world, but that was because she'd only seen him from afar and he almost always had his sweatshirt hood up. Maybe he thought that made him look tough. Or maybe he didn't want to be seen. Whatever. But if looking tough was his goal, Kate thought, he spoiled it with those dark-framed glasses that looked about twenty years out of fashion.

So, yeah, he seemed a little geeky, Kate decided, but minus the glasses, more just like a regular kid. From what she could see, his most outstanding feature, besides the glasses, was his upper lip, which had the hint of a mustache that didn't appear intentional, but suggested maybe his father hadn't bought him a razor yet.

"Hooper, I want to talk to you," Kate said. She tried to make eye contact, but Hooper's eyes darted back and forth between Curtis and the floor as if Kate wasn't even there.

"Hooper?"

He took a step back.

Had she scared him? She tried again, softening her voice in case she had sounded too aggressive. "Hooper, look, you and me and Curtis, we've got to stop."

Hooper's eyes flashed a killer look at Curtis. "Where's the paper?" he asked quickly.

Curtis nodded toward Kate.

"That's what I'm trying to tell you," Kate said. "There is no paper today. I'm not cheating for you anymore."

"Yeah. I'm out of it, too," Curtis added, holding up his hands. "It's over, Hoop."

Hooper kept backing up.

"Stop!" Kate urged him. "Come on. We need to talk. And you need to return my journal."

At that, Hooper spun on his heel and took off.

"Don't go! *Please* don't go!" Kate begged, running a few steps after him. She had put a lot of thought into what she was going to say. *We need to forgive each other. We need to put this behind us. We all need to start over.*

"Don't screw up, Hooper!" Curtis yelled after him.

Astonished at how quickly it had deteriorated, Kate's mouth dropped, and her hands fell to her sides. She turned to Curtis. "What do you think he's going to do?"

Curtis threw up his hands and let them drop. "No idea. Fifty-fifty chance he does nothing."

Which meant a fifty-fifty chance he *would* do something.

"I just wanted to talk to him," Kate said, frustrated at Hooper's reaction. "He didn't even give me a chance."

"I told you. He doesn't do so well with talking," Curtis said. "But I'll try to get to him today."

"You won't fight or anything, will you?"

Curtis almost laughed. "No. That's not Hooper's style."

Kate was unsettled, but they both needed to get to class.

At lunchtime, Kate rushed to her locker to retrieve her cell phone. She turned her back to the stream of kids rushing to lunch and brought up Facebook. Quickly, she typed in the name of Curtis's brother, Justin Jenkins. Sure enough, a page came up. NO HERO it said across the top. Below was a picture of Justin in his army uniform. And below that, a simple declarative sentence: *Justin Jenkins killed himself.*

That was it. A small page Hooper must have made and had ready to launch. A page that people would not see unless they looked for it! And why would they look for it? Kids at Corsica High wouldn't, because no one in the school knew Justin Jenkins! Hooper hadn't even made the connection to Curtis. The whole thing was so stupid.

She sent a text to Curtis.

Kate: *Did you see the Facebook page?*

Curtis: *Yeah, i saw it.*

Kate: *But no one else will! No one cares. Ignore it.*

Kate waited, but Curtis did not text back. She'd been too quick with her words. Of course someone cared—Curtis cared. She hoped he didn't take her comments the wrong way. She tried to text again, but no reply. Did the appearance of a Facebook page about Justin mean that Hooper was going to follow through on the other threats? Was he going to call Valley

Shore or make a Facebook page and report Kate's secret flock and J.T.'s project?

Cell phones were supposed to be kept in lockers all day, but Kate put her phone on mute and hid it in her purse. She kept checking, but no messages came. In Creative Writing class, Curtis didn't even show up. As if to rub it all in, Mr. Ellison's writing prompt was the word *regret*.

Kate covered her eyes to make it look like she was contemplating an interesting idea, but she was too consumed with worry to write anything clever. She would need to move the chicks, but where? Should she call J.T. to warn him? Should she alert her mother? Should she fake a stomachache and beg to go home?

No, she decided. She needed to chill, because Hooper might not do anything. There was still a chance for it to blow over. It was one thing to create a Facebook page on the computer and quite another to actually make a phone call to a company. She doubted Hooper would be that bold. He could barely talk to her. How would he muster the courage to talk to a strange grown-up?

Never had there been a longer school day. Every ten minutes, Kate snuck a look at her phone. No messages. When the bus finally dropped her off at home, the anxiety only increased, because a strange car was in the yard.

Kate's mother met her in the driveway with a worried look on her face. "Kate, two men from Valley Shore are here. They heard you were keeping some of their chicks at an abandoned farm next door."

Kate froze. Hooper had made the call.

"I don't know what they heard, or how," Mom continued in a hurried, low voice. "I told them I didn't know anything. I figured maybe when they realize it's just a kid, they won't make a big deal out of it."

Kate bit her lip, listening.

"When we get over there, let them see for themselves and just tell them the truth," her mother advised. "Tell them the same way you told me."

"Okay." She nodded. She would tell them the truth and take the blame and hope the company did not come down hard on her mother for what she'd done.

"And listen," Kate's mother added, touching her arm and speaking softly. "J.T. doesn't know these men are here. I didn't want to get him upset."

Kate hung her head. If the company knew about the chicks, then surely they knew about J.T.'s project, too. That would be next.

After putting her backpack inside, Kate walked with her mother to the car. She got into the backseat with her mother, and introductions were quickly made. A Mr. Nevill from the company, the driver, did the talking while Mr. Hornbeck had opened the car door for them.

"It's illegal, you know, to take chickens from the company. If you were not culling properly, that's against policy as well," Mr. Nevill said.

Kate sat without expression. Neither she nor her mother said anything.

"Let's go check it out and see what we've got," Mr. Nevill said.

Sitting in the backseat of a strange car that smelled like stale cigarette smoke, Kate felt her downfall was nearly complete. Maybe she had helped J.T., but in the process, she'd become a liar and a cheat, an eavesdropper, a bad friend, and a mediocre student. Now it would be her fault if the farm lost its contract, and she would have destroyed her brother's project.

Kate pressed her lips together and held her mother's hand tightly. She didn't see any way out. As the car drove up Beck's bumpy, overgrown driveway, it was apparent that a vehicle had been on the property recently. When the car stopped, Kate and her mother followed the two men down the path through tall grass that Kate and Curtis had created when they hauled in the feed bag. Tears gathered in Kate's eyes. In addition to her own downfall, she knew the men would simply take all the chicks and kill them.

Oddly, the door to the coop was open. When the two men disappeared inside, Kate glanced quizzically at her mother. "Did you do something?"

"No!" she whispered. "I had no idea these people were coming!"

Kate wiped at her eyes, then she and her mother followed the men inside the coop and stopped, astonished.

The coop was empty. Not a chicken in it. Even the bag of feed and the water jugs were gone. Kate glanced at the spot where an animal had almost dug a hole to get inside, but the board she had used was exactly where she had left it.

It was obvious, however, that chickens had been there. White feathers and chicken manure covered the floor.

Mr. Nevill turned to Kate. "Where are they?"

Stunned, Kate turned to her mother, who shrugged, then looked back at Mr. Nevill. "I told you. We don't know what you're talking about."

Back at the house, the two company men stood in the yard with stern looks and hands on their hips—like referees who couldn't decide on a call.

"I don't know what happened with those chicks," Mr. Nevill said loudly in order to be heard over the noise of the combine harvesting soybeans. "But we also have information about your son, Mrs. Tyler. We understand he's doing a project for school that involves testing your chicken manure for arsenic."

"He *is*?" Kate's mother was genuinely surprised.

Frowning, Mr. Hornbeck crossed his arms as Mr. Nevill continued. "We hear he has collected samples from three different farms, including this one."

"Well, let me stop you right there," Kate's mother declared in an equally loud voice. "Because I thought that chicken manure belonged to the farmer. That it was ours because the company did not want the responsibility for getting rid of it."

Mr. Nevill glared at Kate's mother and had to wait a few seconds until the nearby combine turned a corner and started moving away from the house. "If we find out your son is testing chicken manure from this farm for arsenic, or for anything else, we will shut you down so fast you won't know what happened."

Kate knew he wasn't kidding, and in that moment, it struck her how much power the company had over their lives. It wasn't just the chickens, but the crops, too. All the soybeans being harvested at that very moment would be trucked to a mill *owned by the chicken company.* Just like their corn and the final price paid for their chicken meat, the company would determine the value of the soybeans.

Kate's mother was not intimidated by the company men. She put her own hands on her hips. "What have you got to fear, Mr. Nevill? Valley Shore says it hasn't put arsenic in the chicken feed for years. Why would you worry?"

Inwardly, Kate was beaming. *Go, Mom!* she silently cheered.

"Do I need to repeat myself?" Mr. Nevill asked. "If we find out your son is testing chicken manure, we will shut you down. We have plenty of different ways to do it. Am I making myself clear, Mrs. Tyler?"

Kate's eyes widened. Amazed, she thought, *Who is the bully now?*

~28~
RUFFLING FEATHERS

That night, Uncle Ray came over to help them figure out what to do. With his arm still cradled in a sling, he sat in the living room armchair surrounded by Kate's family, including J.T., who lay on the couch with his injured leg on a pillow. Only Kerry was missing, but she was just outside playing on the swings with her three cousins.

"Let's go over it again," Uncle Ray said. "The company pretty much let the issue of the chicks go, since they didn't find any of them, right?" He didn't wait for an answer, but his eyes flicked over to Kate. "I don't think I want to know too much more about that one," he said, thankfully letting the subject drop.

Her uncle cleared his throat. "The company also said that if J.T. completes his project involving the testing of chicken manure for arsenic, they would shut you down."

"That's it," Kate's mother confirmed. "That's what he said."

Uncle Ray turned to J.T. "Is it worth it, son," he asked, "to put your family's farm in jeopardy for the sake of a school project?"

J.T. sat up and looked stunned. "Is that what this is all about? Wow. Why didn't you tell me earlier? How did they even get wind of that?"

Kate quickly averted her eyes.

"I had to give up on that project!" J.T. exclaimed. "I can't test the chicken manure! The testing is too sophisticated—and way too expensive for a kid like me. But I would have done it if I could have!"

"J.T., I think you need to assume that if it's illegal to put arsenic in chicken feed, the companies are complying with the law."

"No one is doing regular tests, though!" J.T. argued. "I just wanted to find out for sure."

"But *why*?" Uncle Ray asked.

J.T. paused before answering. "Because I was angry. I still am. Because even if there is a state law banning arsenic in feed now, it was new in 2012. There wasn't a law for a lot of years. A long time ago, when Dad was hauling his own feed bags and slitting them open with his jackknife, he was probably inhaling that stuff. He told me himself one day he wondered if that dust could have given him the cancer."

Silence.

"He never mentioned that to me," Uncle Ray said, his voice barely above a whisper.

Kate's mother leaned forward. "No. I never heard that either."

"That's because Dad didn't want you to worry," J.T. told them. "Anyway, no one could ever know for sure if the two things were linked."

Kate watched her mother's face droop with sadness. Were they all thinking the same thing? How in this very room they had moved in a hospital bed for the last month of her father's life? The couch had to be carried into the dining room to make space, and the bed never did look right, pushed up against the wall beneath a narrow wooden shelf displaying her mother's pretty china teacups. Kate stared at the spot where an IV pole had replaced her father's reading lamp and a TV tray by the bed had always been littered with wadded tissues and medicine bottles.

"Look," J.T. continued in a softer voice, "I'm not doing the chicken manure thing, because I can't. I shifted gears. The federal Food and Drug Administration banned arsenic in chicken feed nationwide the year after Maryland—in 2013. So maybe we don't have to worry about it anymore. Although who knows? Plus, I've read that they can still give it to turkeys."

"Well, we don't raise turkeys," Uncle Ray said.

"Tell them about the antibiotics," Kate urged her brother.

"That's what I want to focus on," J.T. said. "Feed companies can put antibiotics in the chicken feed if they say they're treating sick chickens. But a lot of them could be doing it just to make the chickens grow faster."

"And what's wrong with that?" Uncle Ray asked.

"What's wrong is we could be creating all this antibiotic-resistant bacteria. It could get passed on to humans through chicken meat! You could get sick from it, but there wouldn't be a medicine to cure you. You could die!"

"Do you think there could be antibiotics in our chicken feed now?" J.T.'s mother asked.

J.T. shrugged. "Mom, we've never known what's in the feed. For years it was arsenic. I read a report that said chicken farmers in other countries used stuff like Benadryl, Tylenol, and Prozac to keep chickens calm because if they're stressed, they grow slower. Another report says they fed them coffee pulp and green tea to keep them awake so they'd eat more."

Uncle Ray was shaking his head. "I don't know a chicken farmer around here who would feed that stuff to his birds."

"Probably not! But still, they don't know what's in the feed, Uncle Ray! By contract, the company provides the feed! You can't ask questions about it! You can't ask questions about hardly anything about the chicken business 'cause of politics and state laws. It's called 'agricultural secrecy.' There's a lot we don't know. Like about all that chicken manure running off into the water. People like us—the public—we can't even read the reports about it!" As he spoke, he struggled to sit up on the couch.

"J.T., calm down," Grandma warned, reaching over to put a hand on his shoulder. "You're going to hurt that leg!"

"Where are you getting this information?" Uncle Ray pressed him.

"Lots of places," J.T. said. "I read reports online, and I've been e-mailing with a researcher at the Bloomberg School of Public Health at Johns Hopkins University."

Uncle Ray rubbed his forehead. "*Whew!* I don't know what you're getting yourself into with all this, J.T. I understand why it's important. But I also know Valley Shore won't like you shining a light on their business and making some kind of poster about it at the school fair, where the local press will pick up on it. I'm telling you, the company won't stand for it. You ruffle their feathers, and they *will* shut you down. And I'll bet your dad has two or three hundred thousand dollars invested in those two buildings and all the equipment."

"Two hundred thousand," Kate's mother clarified.

"There you go. That's a big chunk of change," Uncle Ray declared. "The bank loaned your family that money, and you all have to pay it back. How else are you going to do it without the income from the chickens?"

"They're like bullies!" Kate interjected. "The chicken companies are like bullies to all the chicken farmers, aren't they? Do this. Do that. Do it our way, or we'll cancel your contract and put you out of business!"

A brief pause. Nobody disagreed.

"Be practical. You've got to protect yourselves," Uncle Ray said. "You and the Richards family down the way, the Masons, the Franklins. You're all good people, working hard, just trying to make a living. *It's a business.* There's a lot of money and powerful people behind Valley Shore. You can't fight them and expect to win."

"You're probably right," J.T. admitted. He looked across the table at Kate's mother. "I'll let it go if you want, Mom. I sure don't want to get us in trouble. But someday I'm going to follow up on this. I know now that there are people who study these issues and put pressure on the government to change the laws. That's what I want to do. It's not fair what these big companies and factory farms get away with—it's not right! People deserve to know what they're buying—and what they're *eating.*

"Maybe this is what I'll do for my job one day. Do research like that scientist I e-mailed," J.T. declared. Then he added softly, "I'll do it for Dad."

Kate blinked her moist eyes. She felt so proud of J.T., and so guilty for her role in exposing his project, which he was now giving up.

"No," Kate's mother declared.

Everyone looked at her.

She shook her head. "No. You should continue with your project, J.T. You have a right to research and write a paper for school on these issues." She tapped a finger on the coffee table to make her point. "If Valley Shore has a problem with that, let them cancel our contract."

Uncle Ray winced. "But *that's* not practical!"

Kate's mother held up a hand to stop him. "I've got some life insurance money that Jacob left us."

It was the first anyone had heard about life insurance.

"How much, Angela? Can you tell us?" Uncle Ray asked.

"The policy is for one hundred thousand dollars," she said.

"But that would barely cover half of your mortgage," Uncle Ray noted.

"Yes, but we have some savings, too. Things would be tight, there's no question, but maybe this is the change we all need."

J.T. and Kate widened their eyes.

Uncle Ray leaned back in his chair.

"The more I think about it, the more I think it's time for us to get out of this business," Kate's mother went on. "Maybe we should just pay off the mortgage and try something else."

"Like *what*?" Kate asked.

"Well. We'd own these chicken houses. We could raise chickens for the eggs. People want cage-free and free-range eggs. We could do that."

J.T. tried to sit up again. "*Mom?*"

"It's just a suggestion," she said, with a wan smile.

"But we could all help!" Kate said eagerly.

"Absolutely!" J.T. agreed.

In that quiet moment when everyone was absorbing the refreshing idea of a new business—a whole new beginning—Kate heard the *ding* of a text arriving. While the others were talking, she pulled the phone from her pocket and read the message:

Curtis: *So how much do I feed these guys?*

~29~
MAYBE

Weeks went by. The jack-o'-lanterns on the porch steps rotted, sank in on themselves, and had to be tossed. The leaves had fallen, and the trees were mostly skinny and bare, although from the back upstairs bedrooms, a view of the river was possible now. Geese were still picking through the harvested cornfields, but the soybean fields lay flat and brown under an often cloudy November sky the color of slate.

J.T. progressed from the wheelchair to crutches, but his injured leg remained weak, and he tired easily. Doctors advised him not to go back to school until after the holidays.

"You are joining the marching band, no question about it," Ashley kept telling him when she stopped by with books and homework assignments. But despite her unflagging optimism, a doctor had warned J.T. that he might always have a significant limp.

The chicken feed project was put on hold, too, so J.T. could focus on makeup work and physical therapy. Valley Shore and the Tylers, by mutual agreement, ended their contract anyway. Kate's mother paid off the mortgage, but borrowing money to start a new business wasn't so easy, and the chicken houses remained empty.

Brady came over one Saturday afternoon. The two boys pulled an old video game called *Star Craft* off the shelf in J.T.'s closet and spent hours together building space civilizations. Kate was amazed—and delighted. She surprised them by making their favorite nachos, melting cheese over corn chips in the microwave. It was like nothing had ever happened between the two boys. Too good to be true, Kate thought. And it was—because weeks went by after that visit, and Brady never came again, not even over Thanksgiving vacation when everyone had five days off. Neither did he call or text.

"I guess he's not over it either," J.T. told Uncle Ray one evening when he and Aunt Helen brought the girls for cake and ice cream to celebrate Kerry's seventh birthday. They were the only two left in the living room after the party. The girls had all run outside despite the chilly December evening to see Kerry's new bike, and the others were cleaning up in the kitchen. Kate just happened to overhear because she was putting things away in the pantry, a small narrow room between the kitchen and the living room.

"Truth is," Uncle Ray said to J.T., "none of you boys will ever be *over* it. You all have to learn how to live *with* it. You and Brady—Digger, too."

Kate froze with a box of tea in her hands upon hearing Digger's name. He was the friend most responsible for sabotaging the red kayak that had caused so much tragedy.

"Digger will be home soon, I hear, and then you three will have to figure out the next step," Uncle Ray continued. "In answer to your question, though, I don't know if a real friendship is ever possible again. Maybe—if you find a way to forgive one another. But for sure you got to give it more time. If it's gonna work, you'll have to ease back into the friendship slowly."

It gave Kate goose bumps listening to her uncle. Her eyes teared up, too, because he sounded just like their father. Uncle Ray's advice was the kind of advice Dad would have given J.T. if he were here. She put a hand on her heart.

"Thanks, Uncle Ray," J.T. said. "Thanks for talking with me about it. It's been hard. Real hard . . ."

When J.T.'s voice broke, Kate looked down, almost ashamed to be listening.

"Don't you ever think twice about it," Uncle Ray told him. "It's what family's for. I'm here for you guys. You know that."

Grandma and Kate's grandfather both came up to Maryland for Christmas. But there was one more visitor before J.T. returned to school after the holidays. Curtis stopped by.

From the kitchen window, Kate watched him walk down the hill to the shed where J.T. was changing the oil on one of the tractors. They were in the shed together for a long time while Kate stood staring at the two pairs of tracks the boys had made through the snow. Because he still used crutches, J.T.'s tracks were a mess of lines and boot prints, but the snow didn't stop him, or slow him down, and neither did his injured leg. Kate hoped Curtis had come to deliver the long-awaited apology, but when she asked J.T. about it later, he didn't want to talk about it.

"Just stuff," he said, stomping snow from his boots. "No big deal."

"Excuse me, *no big deal*?" Kate asked.

J.T. shrugged and hobbled over to the sink to wash the oil off his hands. Kate figured he wasn't going to share anything about the visit and started to walk away. But she stopped and swung around when her brother commented, "I told him it was all ancient history."

When J.T. returned to school after the holiday break, Kate stayed by his side, carrying his things. She was surprised to see Brady waiting at her brother's locker. "Here, I'll take his books," Brady said to Kate. He grinned at her when she handed over J.T.'s backpack. "Ashley's going to take over at lunch," he said.

So the boys had been in touch again, even though J.T. never said anything. Kate smiled back at Brady and, too anxious to think clearly, said simply, "That's great."

Brady hoisted J.T.'s backpack over one shoulder, his own backpack over the other, and went to work, clearing the way for J.T. to maneuver his way down the busy hall on crutches. Kate stood watching, wiping at her eyes once, until the two boys, their heads bobbing above the crowd, finally disappeared through the double doors that led upstairs.

Later, when Kate saw Curtis outside the cafeteria, she stopped to thank him for coming over and talking to J.T.

"No problem," he said. "Long overdue." Suddenly, he pulled Kate's missing journal from his pile of books and handed it to her. "I was waiting for a chance to give you this. Got it back from Hooper over the weekend, just before he moved."

Kate hugged the journal to her chest, but her eyes never left Curtis's face. "Hooper *moved*?"

"He went down to Salisbury to be with his mom. She enrolled him in a school down there, where he'll get some kind of special help. He didn't want to talk about it much, but he seemed glad to be going. Anyway, I went over to help him get his things together."

"You did?"

"Yeah. I bagged up all the fish in his aquarium for him. We put them in an insulated cooler for the trip. Then I washed out the aquarium and put it in the back of his mother's car."

"Wow. Mr. Nice Guy," Kate teased.

"Look," Curtis said, leaning in toward Kate, "Hooper never squealed about what we did. We should just move on."

"I suppose," she agreed.

"It's better for J.T., too," Curtis added. "How do you think he'd feel if he knew what we'd done?"

Kate's eyes met his and, somewhat reluctantly, she nodded in agreement.

"So how are my chickens doing?" she asked, eager to change the subject.

"We are really enjoying the eggs!" he told her. "My mother's boyfriend, especially. Ol' Zeke really got into it. He's the one who built most of that new coop, you know. He takes care of those chickens more than I do. You need to come over and see them one day."

"I will," Kate promised.

Things were looking up again. Hooper was gone, J.T. was back in school, and Jess had a little surprise of her own. "You were right about the cheating," she said to Kate one morning on the bus.

Kate whirled around to face her. "What?"

Jess looked down. "Yeah. You said I was cheating myself, or something like that, by not being true to myself and giving up Quote of the Day."

"I did?" Relieved, Kate let her breath out. "I said that?"

"Yeah! 'Time discovers the truth,'" Jess said, smiling.

Kate frowned, confused.

"'Time discovers the truth'—it's my first quote!" Jess explained. "It's from a Roman philosopher named Seneca. I have my old job back!"

Kate beamed. "I am *really* glad, Jess!"

"Yeah. I needed to do it for myself. Especially after I found out the truth about how much Olivia was making fun of me. Not just to my face either, but behind my back!"

"That wasn't very nice," Kate said.

"No. I mean, she did say she was sorry, and I think we're still friends. But still. She didn't have much respect for what was important to me. It made me look at her a little differently."

Kate didn't say anything, but as the school bus rumbled on and she turned her attention forward again, she had to wonder deep inside about Jess's new quote. Was time going to discover the truth of what Kate had done? And if people, including Jess, found out about the cheating, would they understand? Would they look at her differently?

On the home front, things took another step forward when Kate's mother was able to obtain a loan from the bank so she could start a new business.

Maybe things would finally get back to normal, Kate thought. Maybe.

"I thought we'd visit Arlington National Cemetery at Easter when Grandma and Grandpa come back up," Kate's mother said one evening at dinner. "We could take some of the early blooming daffodils down by the tractor shed. Dad always liked those—the yellow ones with orange centers. And J.T.'s never seen the grave." She glanced at her son across the table, and her voice grew soft. "I'm so sorry I didn't allow you to come that day."

J.T. shrugged. "It's okay, Mom," he said, briefly catching Kate's eyes. Some things, they both seemed to agree, were better left unsaid.

~30~
SECRETS

They arrived on a warm spring day in late March. A Saturday, as it turned out, so Kate, J.T., and Kerry were able to go, too, when the post office called.

"We'll be right over to pick them up," Kate's mother said.

They left the breakfast dishes until later and jumped in the family van. Kate's mother drove.

As soon as J.T. opened the heavy glass door to the post office, they could hear them peeping. Two women at the front window chuckled.

"Not every day we get a delivery like this!" the woman on duty commented. She hustled into the back to get the first of several shipping crates with the noisy cargo and brought it out front to the lobby, where she carefully set it down on the floor.

Kate's family bent over to peek in at the newborn chicks through the many breathing holes on each side of the crate. More and more cartons joined the first one, and soon the small post office lobby was awash in a cacophony of peeps!

A woman with a package in her arms paused to look, and a man getting his mail came over to see. "How many chicks?" he asked.

"Five hundred Rhode Island reds," Kate's mother said. And Kate thought she said it rather proudly.

"They came overnight from New Mexico!" Kerry added, clapping her small hands in excitement. "They flew on an airplane!"

"What do you know," another customer chuckled. "Rhode Island chickens from New Mexico!"

"They didn't need food and water?" someone asked.

"Just hatched, they can go for seventy-two hours without food and water," J.T. explained. "It's because they're still ingesting their yolk sacs. It's all the nourishment they need."

Kate shook her head and smiled. Leave it to her brainy brother to know something like that.

Back at the Tylers' farm, one of the chicken houses had been prepared for its new inhabitants. The floors were scraped and scrubbed clean. The feeders and drinkers were filled with starter feed and water. Perches for sleeping at night were set up, and lines of cozy boxes for egg-laying were installed above conveyor belts that would gather and move the eggs. While the windows and doors were closed for the time being, they would be open soon so the growing chicks could go outside during the day into a huge grassy yard that had been enclosed with electric fencing. Small benches were in place so the chickens would have shade, and several shiny CDs were hung on strings as modern-day scarecrows to frighten away predators like hawks and eagles with their bright reflections.

Everyone was onboard for the new journey.

About the same time the new chicks arrived, Kate and Jess began softball practice after school—and Jess got her braces off. "Look at these teeth!" she kept saying, thrusting her toothy smiles at Kate. "I was gorgeous under all that wire, but no one knew it!"

Kate laughed. "Your modesty surprises me!" she said sarcastically.

"Time discovers the truth," Jess said. "Remember?"

"Time is not the only thing that discovers the truth. Jeffrey Brown discovered your true beauty, too," Kate quipped.

"Oh, my gosh, he is so incredibly sweet," Jess said. "But you should talk! I know Brady's been helping you with math."

"Just a little."

Jess narrowed her eyes with concern. "Hey, what happened to your arm?"

Kate glanced at the pink blotch of skin below her wrist and rolled her eyes. "Burned it on my flat iron."

Jess's face melted into a silly smile as she poked Kate in the ribs. "I thought you didn't like using that hair straightener!"

Despite all the new beginnings, Kate struggled inside. The cheating hung on her like a heavy, but invisible, tattered coat. No one else could see it, but Kate knew the ugly thing was there, and it weighed her down.

She often thought back to her father's funeral and J.T.'s secret playing of the trumpet for taps. *No one else knew . . . No one else would ever need to know*. And she wondered, why not regard the cheating in the same way? Did anyone need to know? If so, then *why*? What difference would it make *now*?

Everybody had secrets, Kate told herself. Her grandmother once said that before she died, she hoped she would know the secret about who really was behind the assassination of President John F. Kennedy. Her family would likely never learn the details of her father's war injury, because he had never wanted to talk about it. Nor would they ever know if it was malevolent dust from chicken feed that had caused his kidney cancer. Curtis would always wonder why his brother had killed himself. And, Kate couldn't help but think, unless scientists—or people like J.T.—did research to check up on factory farm secrets, people would never know what they were eating!

Why couldn't Kate's cheating be one of those things people didn't know? J.T. wasn't bullied anymore. The bullying had been cruel and unfair, and she had stopped it. Didn't the ends justify the means? Kate wanted to think so, but she couldn't be sure. There didn't seem to be a black or white answer. And that reminded her of something.

Her mind drifted back to the day their father had shown J.T. how to do the culling and she had run away, unable to watch anymore. That night, when she and J.T. were sitting on the roof, Dad had startled them by squeezing through the bedroom window to join them. He was a big man, and it wasn't easy for him, especially with his bum knee, but he pulled through anyway, scraping his work shoes against the shingles. He plunked himself down heavily between the two of them and put a thick arm around each.

"I wanted to tell you something," he said. "I wanted to tell you that there are a lot of times in life when you're not sure what's right and what's wrong. A lot of things aren't pure black and white, and that's because people look at things different. There's a lot of gray areas out there. So sometimes, you listen to your heart, and sometimes, you listen to your head because you have to be practical. You have to respect how others feel, too. But then you do the best you can, not only for yourself, but for your family."

Of course, Dad had been talking about killing chickens, not cheating at school, but Kate seriously wondered if it came down to the same thing.

Time discovers the truth. Should she confess before it caught up with her?

Her head said yes, but her heart said, no.

During the last week of school, Kate saw an opportunity. She and J.T. had stayed after school for Kate's last softball game. J.T. had hurt his leg again trying to do too much too fast and was back on crutches. The plan was that after the game, they would clean out his locker, and Kate would carry a box of his things out to their mother's van. Kate was in the hallway, heading to J.T.'s locker, when she passed the main office and saw the principal standing at the front counter with a teacher.

Still in her softball uniform, Kate stopped and shifted the duffel bag on her shoulder. She had been thinking more and more about talking to Mrs. Larkin before school ended. The timing was good, she figured, because a whole long summer stretched before them—plenty of time to forget, and forgive. She had just turned fourteen, but she already knew, thanks to

Brady and her brother, that time had a way of softening the edges, however sharp they once had been.

Turning her head, Kate could see J.T. far down the hallway, kneeling in front of his locker and pulling things out. The principal, meanwhile, ended her conversation with the teacher and was walking away.

Surely Mrs. Larkin would give Kate a minute. She might even invite Kate into her office to sit down. It wouldn't take long. Kate knew how she'd begin the conversation, because she had already written the first words in her head. All she had to do was repeat them.

At the beginning of ninth grade, I cheated. I wrote an essay in Creative Writing for Curtis Jenkins. I wrote papers assigned in English and ancient history for Hooper Delaney. I did it so those boys would leave my brother, J.T., alone and give him a chance to start over. It worked. I know that doesn't make what I did right . . .

J.T. was standing up in front of his locker, getting the crutches back under his arms.

The principal disappeared into her office, but her door was still open.

J.T. held his hands palm up, like *what's going on?*

Still Kate hesitated. How would she ever finish that confession? Because bottom line, no matter how many times she went over it in her mind, she could be certain of only two things:

She loved her family.

And she was not sorry she had cheated.

Given the same situation, she would do it again.

"Kate, are you coming?" J.T. called to her, his voice echoing against the locker-lined walls.

She swallowed hard. Should she ask him to wait a minute?

Impatient, her brother started to set his crutches against the wall so he could bend down and pick up the box himself.

Two days of school remained. There would be another chance.

"J.T., wait! I'm coming!" Kate called, turning, walking, and then almost running to help her brother.

Acknowledgments

For information on the poultry business, I wish to thank Carole Morison, a former chicken farm owner and now agricultural consultant; researchers, especially Dr. Keeve Nachman, at the Johns Hopkins Center for a Livable Future, the Johns Hopkins Bloomberg School of Public Health in Baltimore; and Maryland delegate Tom Hucker who, with his staff, worked tirelessly to get Maryland to be the first state in the country to ban arsenic-containing antibiotics from chicken feed in 2012.

I am also grateful to teachers and students at Chesapeake High School in Pasadena, Maryland, for letting me hang out with them; to Melissa Porter, a probation officer in the Kent County, Maryland, department of juvenile services; and to our family friend, Dee Davis, farmer extraordinaire, who showed me how to operate a tractor and a Bush Hog. As always, I am grateful to my husband and first reader, John; my son, Will, for his technical advice; and my daughter, Hannah, for her help and inspiration.

ALSO BY
PRISCILLA CUMMINGS:

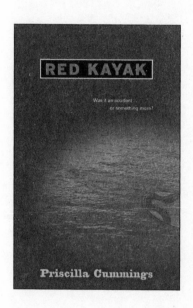